D0049258

The Royal Diaries

ELIZABETH I

Red Rose
of the
House of Tudor

BY KATHRYN LASKY

Scholastic Inc. New York

England, 1544

July 1, 1544
Greenwich Palace

I am a forgotten Princess.

At times my father, King Henry VIII, needs to forget me. When the King needs to forget, the whole court follows suit and I am usually exiled to Hatfield. I don't mind. Hatfield is lovely. It is more of a mansion than a Palace, cozy, red brick with a huge forested hunting park. But when one is in exile, one is not treated the same. Everything is different.

Now, thank goodness, I am back at Court after nearly a year of being banished. The dear Queen, Catherine Parr, convinced my father to bring me back from Hatfield. She told him that he must see me before he goes off to France. She is very kind, this new mother of mine.

Kat, my governess, gave me this diary just this morning. It is bound in leather and embossed with the Tudor rose, the symbol of my family. As soon as I opened it and touched its creamy white pages, I knew that it was the perfect companion for me, a forgotten Princess. Within these leather covers I can commit my most private and utmost secret thoughts. It is here that I shall speak my mind. There will be no flourishes of words and language. I shall call the King Father, for that is what he is, and not use language such as Sire and Your Majesty, the way one must write in letters or speak in Court.

And because these thoughts are so secret, they must never be read and forever be hidden. Here, at Greenwich Palace, there is a loose stone under the bed in my chamber where I shall keep this diary. But I live in many palaces, as the court is always moving. So I must find equally secret places wherever I am. My candle burns down low. I do not know why they give me these short, slender candles. I need some of those fat tapers they use to light the hallways and corridors. My chamber is so large here, too large really to be cozy. The candle casts the smallest pool of light. I write by a narrow slit of a window through which only a piece of the moon can shine and a single star. So I must blow out the candle and wait for the break of day and new light.

Good night.

July 2, 1544

The light this early in the morning is pink and is enough by which to read and write. But to whom am I writing here on this blank page? To whom am I speaking when I speak to an empty piece of vellum?

Do you know who I am? I shall tell you. I am Elizabeth, Princess of England, daughter of Henry VIII and his wife Anne Boleyn. I am eleven years old. My mother, once Queen, is now dead. Almost eight years ago, when I was not yet three, Father chopped off her head. Not he himself. He ordered it done. Indeed, he sent for a French swordsman. They are skilled in beheading, and it hurts less with a sword than with an ax, or so they say. It is not as if anyone has come back to speak on the matter.

I hear Kat rustling in the adjoining chamber. The servitor has come with breakfast no doubt. I hope it is not the cold rabbit pie again. I am sick to death of rabbit pie. I am not hungry anywise. I am by my window, watching Father mount his horse and take a turn in the yard below. Father is quite, no, very fat. Because of his weight and the terrible sores that afflict his legs and make them swell, he can no longer mount a horse by himself. He requires four attendants and a crane to get him onto his horse in full armor. It is almost as exciting as watching a tournament to see him being cranked up and then lowered onto his horse.

Later

It was rabbit pie, but Kat didn't make me eat it. She didn't eat it, either. She sniffed it in that special way she has. The very tip of her long bony nose takes on a life of its own and begins to twitch. Then the fatal words: It is off. "Off" means rancid, spoiled. So we just ate cheese and bread and drank cider.

In two days' time, Father leaves for France, which he is invading. He will ride to Dover and then cross the Channel to Calais. Her Majesty Catherine Parr, his sixth wife, promises that she will do all she can to permit us, the children, to accompany the royal party as far as Dover so we can see him off. That will be an even greater spectacle with ten thousand men and drummers and trumpeters.

Oh! Oh! Finally, Father is on the horse! He canters off round the yard. "Hooray! Hooray!" they all cry. Then, "Hal! Hal!" My father's fool, Will Somers, shouts. Will is the only one to call him Hal. Yes, he is a sight, my father. The sun glints off his armor. He is like a mountain of silver — gleaming and huge.

July 3, 1544

So, dear diary, I read my last words, My father glints like a mountain of silver. And I, looking down upon him yesterday, was like a slim shadow in the window. For you see I am not only often forgotten but nearly invisible. I promised I would tell you all. Well, here is the start of my story of invisibility, of being forgotten.

I have had five mothers in all. I have liked them all. I did not know the first of my father's six wives. But I have liked all the others. They do, however, run together in my head. I barely remember Jane Seymour, Prince Edward's mother. I was but four when she died. I cannot talk of Catherine Howard. She was so beautiful and young. More like a playmate than a mother. But I cannot bear to tell of her end, not now at least. It was too awful. I was old enough to remember, unlike with my mother.

Just before Catherine Howard, there was Anne of Cleves. A very jolly sort. She is German and speaks in great guttural gushes often spraying spit. That and the fact she looks like a horse, or so my father said, made for a very short marriage. Father "un-wifed" her. He does not like the term "divorce." But they are friends still, rather like sister and brother. She is here now at Greenwich and shall go to Dover with all of us. It will be a jolly affair sending Father off to war. Really jolly if Princess Mary wouldn't come. I do wish that as sisters Princess Mary and I were as fond of each other as Father and his "sister" Anne of Cleves. Princess Mary is twenty-eight, and all she ever does is pray, and she never smiles.

Father likes to forget Princess Mary sometimes, too, for she reminds him of his first wife, Catherine of Aragon. Somewhere between all these wives I became invisible, because I was part of something he wanted very badly to forget, too. He likes to think, or indeed he passes decrees that say, that Mary and I are bastards, children of what he insists were illegal marriages, and therefore we could never be Queens of England and rule.

But Catherine Parr changed all that. Now it is said that when Father dies Edward, our little brother, who is just six, shall become King. Then if Edward dies, Princess Mary will be Queen, and if Mary dies, I shall rule. This will not happen. I am third in line and Edward seems healthy to me, although Father thinks Edward is too fat! Is that not funny? My father is the fattest person in the realm and he is calling Edward, who is a trifle plump, fat. Some might think our family is quite confused or mad. That last sentence could be considered treasonous. The punishment for treason is beheading. And I for one would find a French swordsman little comfort. You see why I must hide you.

That, in short, is my story of how I became invisible. I doubt I shall ever be Queen, for it is very difficult for an invisible Princess to wear a crown. I suppose by the same token it might be difficult to behead an invisible Princess. But I am my father's daughter. I do look the most like him and though I am not nearly of his size, I am of his stature. One does not have to be huge to have a stature and a bearing that is royal. Mary does not. Edward, well, Edward is so frail, even if Father thinks he's too fat. I <u>want</u> to be Queen. I think I am smart enough to be Queen. I <u>know</u> I am smart enough. This is not pride. I simply know what I know. But what does it all mean if I remain a slim shadow in a Palace window?

July 4, 1544

I cannot believe what has happened. I am not to go to Dover. I am to be sent forthwith to Hatfield. Everyone else is going — Prince Edward, Princess Mary, Anne of Cleves, the Queen and all her ladies, and dear Robin Dudley! My time at Hatfield would be so much more cheerful if Robin were there, but why should he suffer for me? Robin is my best friend. He is the son of John Dudley, one of my father's closest advisers in the Privy Council and, in fact, commander of the fleet in the campaign against France. So of course he would not miss a chance to see his father off and his father would not banish him like mine has just done to me! Robin dreams, I am sure, of going on campaign someday against the French. It is every knight's dream, and Robin will be a knight, more surely than I shall ever be Queen.

Here is what happened. It was last evening and we were all in the Great Hall for a festive banquet, the last before the campaign. My father likes his amusements, so Will Somers, his fool, had come to tell each of us children to prepare a musical piece to perform. I myself play the table harpsicord — also called the virginal. I usually favor

Father with one of the compositions that he has written, such as "Greensleeves," and then he asks if I have composed anything new. Well, I had, so I played it, but I did not sing the words. "Oh, do sing it, Elizabeth," he said. Well, a King does not have need to press. He commands. So I sang reluctantly, for I knew that the lyrics could be thought of as troublesome. Could — not necessarily would.

Robin clad in green did come to see the queen.
And sitting by the throne
two Princesses were shone.
Hey, nonny, nonny. Hey, nonny, nonny.
One in shadows glowed despite her lack of gems.
The other in the sun looked verily so glum.

Father erupted. He felt the words a terrible insult. That I was fretting about Mary getting to be Queen before myself. That I was an ungrateful wretch! "Enough," he said in that low deadly voice that stops everything. I swear even the birds shut their beaks. A terrible silence descended on the room. It was all I could do to keep from crying. I was sent to my apartments. Half an hour later, Sir Anthony

Denny, a groom of the Privy Chamber, came to inform me that I would be going to Hatfield forthwith.

I knew, of course, before Sir Anthony arrived. Anne of Cleves had followed me out as I left the Great Hall. I felt this spray of spittle on the back of my neck. "I vill speak to him, Elizabeth. I vill try to say something to change his mind. I vill. I vill!"

July 5, 1544

Anne of Cleves came to my apartments today. She could not change his mind. The King's retinue leaves in an hour for Dover. We leave for Hatfield two hours later. I am so sad. My presence is commanded at the east gate as they leave. I shall not deign to record the ceremony and pageantry of their leave taking in this diary. In fact, I shall close my eyes as they pass by.

July 10, 1544
Hatfield

It was quite remarkable; even before we left Greenwich Palace I felt the change. My Ladies of the Chamber, the ones who take care of Kat's and my sewing and laundry, had been reduced from three to one. Instead of three horse grooms, we traveled with one.

The servants who are left us answer less quickly and are often inattentive — sometimes even surly. Why? It's very simple, really. This is not Court. Some even say I am an illegitimate Princess. And then again they listen to all the gossip. You see, they say my mother was a witch. On her left hand she had a sixth finger, just a bit of a nub, naught more. She was always careful to hide it by having her gowns fashioned with long sleeves. But they say it was the mark of a witch. My father says he realized too late that he had been "transfixed" by Anne Boleyn.

So often when my father does look at me, he thinks me half witch. It is a strange predicament, because in many ways I am more like him than either Prince Edward or Princess Mary. We both have red hair, and I, of all the children, have inherited the largest share of his musical talent. I often wonder what he would have felt if I had been born a boy. Would he have then thought me half witch? I was supposed to be a boy. All the astrologers had predicted a boy. The announcements of the birth of a Prince had been engraved. And then I was born. They had to squeeze in two s's. I have a copy of that announcement because of Princess Mary, who gave it to me and kindly pointed out the additional s's.

However, even with two s's, this Princess shall begin to be forgotten again. I shall fade into the dark greenery of the wooded parkland. Oh, to shine as brightly in my father's eyes as Robin does in the eyes of his father.

July 11, 1544

It rains. No playing outdoors. No pony riding or archery practice. Much Greek and Latin. The Queen manages quite well to see to my studies from afar. There is a continual flow of books from her, particularly those on moral philosophy, and I am expected to read them and answer the Queen's questions, write little essays, oftentimes in Greek or Latin. The Queen says she demands much of me because I have a superior intellect. And Kat says that her nurturing of my mind is a sign of true love and devotion, as much as any mother would have for her own daughter. So I vow to work hard. Kat is such a dear, but even Kat now admits that my mastery of Greek and Latin is equal to hers. I practice daily the beautiful Italian script with its lovely loops and flourishes. My handwriting is so spidery when I write in this diary, but I am going to practice my name in the Italian style on this page.

July 12, 1544

Still rains.

July 13, 1544

Still rains. I shall not merely fade and be forgotten — I shall most likely dissolve entirely with this weather.

July 14, 1544

At last, no rain! Rose this morning as usual for Matins at six. I could tell by the Chaplain's voice immediately that the weather was drier. I must admit that in Chapel I was not thinking about God. I was thinking about being

Queen. Not myself, mind you, but Catherine Parr. She is now Queen in more than just title. She is Queen Regent and rules in my father's absence. It is she who must deal with the Privy Chamber councillors and make the decisions. Catherine Parr is so wise and learned, I know she will be a good regent. It saddens me that I cannot be with her now. I enjoy her company and I would like to be near her and see how she talks to the Privy Councillors. [Do they honor her and show respect for her office?] I cannot help but wonder what it might be like being in the Court of a Queen who at this moment in history is the sole ruler of England. There never has been a ruling Queen of England. Just Kings. And if she is the sole ruler, could she not restore me from exile?

July 15, 1544

Kat helps me with my Italian script, but I can teach her something about archery. That is the only thing good about Robin not being here. I am the best archer at Hatfield, I think. Of course, there is hardly anybody here at Hatfield. No children and the barest staff. So it is hardly a competition. I suppose I am the best at Greek and Latin, too, and who knows — maybe the best rider, seeing as none of the King's riding boys are here.

I am so lonely. I wonder if Father ever thinks of me when he is abroad and on campaign. I wonder if I was more lovable as a baby — before I could talk or sing songs with upsetting words. I wish I could remember what it might have been like to be a tiny baby and cradled in his arms, and hear his voice sing a lullaby to me.

July 17, 1544

It seems when one is out of the Court, other things are parceled out in small doses beyond servitors and riding boys — good weather, to be specific. It rains again. A messenger arrived from Westminster Palace and reports it has been nothing but sunny in London. Kat and I play cards and of course there is the interminable needlework. I have at last mastered the backstitch, but I am careful to make a few mistakes because I do not want Kat to advance me yet to the satin stitch. Although needlework is rather mind numbing, when one has a certain level of skill with a particular stitch, one can just do it and still talk. I enjoy so much my conversations with Kat.

For example, tonight when we chatted, I asked her why Master Holbein, the finest Court painter, when sent to paint Anne of Cleves's portrait before my father married her, made her look much fairer in complexion and did not show the pits in her skin. Kat said that Master Holbein never painted pockmarks, and I supposed my father did not think to ask beforehand if she had had the disease. Oh, God, I hope I never do get the smallpox. There is a cook and her daughter at Hampton Court who have pits as big as the holes in the embroidery cloth. Anne of Cleves's pits are not nearly that bad. It was not just the pits, however. It seemed that every bit of Anne of Cleves's appearance offended Father in some way. But my father is no longer such a beauty himself. The last time Holbein painted him, they had to bring up a larger throne, for he did not fit into the one they had planned to use for the portrait. It was a family portrait. Princess Mary and I were left out, which seems odd, seeing as Holbein did include others who were long dead, such as Jane Seymour, Father's fourth wife, and his mother and father. Oh, well, there is no telling with my father. But when his humors are in balance in regard to me, I can honestly say there is no one with whom I would rather be. He can be as playful as a child, full of sport and jest. I just wish he were not so fat.

July 20, 1544

I have thought much in these past few rainy days about the notion of writing the Queen concerning my exile. I prayed this morning in Matins, and the answer came to me with such clarity I know it is right. I may write to Queen Catherine, but I must not put the burden of the decision on her. This would be unfair and could cause for trouble between her and my father. And the very last thing on earth I ever want is trouble between my father and his wife. This I know as well as I know anything. Never again those horrible days at Hampton Court before Catherine Howard's death. I think I should just write to her not as Queen Regent but as my mother, and ask that she make a request to the King on my behalf. Furthermore, I think I should write to her in Italian, as it means so much to her that I master this language and even the script.

July 22, 1544

I am happy for the rainy days as they give me opportunity to work on my letter to the Queen. Kat, by the way, thinks this is an excellent idea. She says she will help me with some of the phrasing, but I do not want her to until I have at least two drafts. The voice must be mine even if it is in Italian — not of course my diary voice, but my respectful daughter-of-the-Court voice.

July 24, 1544

I have a draft of the letter and shall send it soon to Westminster Palace.

July 28, 1544

I received a letter from Princess Mary today. She is full of concern for me and said if it were in her power, she would send one of her Chaplains to assist Chaplain Huntley here at Hatfield. I would rather she sent one of the King's riding boys. How many Chaplains does it take to pray, after all? But, of course, Mary thinks I should pray much more. She writes in her letter, "Dear Sister, What really matters is that God be first in your heart and then you shall be first in <u>His</u>." Then she suggests that I would not mind nor think about this banishment if I would pray more. I would mind just as much!

I come back to that old tiresome quandary. I simply cannot believe that the same father with whom I bowled, scarce a year ago, would now exile me. Mary says that if one prays, one is never an exile in God's heart. I will only confess this to you, dear diary, but in all honesty I do not much care where I am in the Lord's heart. What I really want to know is where am I in my father's?

August 1, 1544

Sent off the letter to Queen Catherine yesterday.

August 7, 1544

Have not written for over a week because the rain stopped, and after all these days of being shut indoors, Kat and I felt compelled to spend every minute outside. The roses in the garden have a touch of rot from the wet weather, but do look glorious on a sunny day. The Tudor rose, which Father insists that every gardener at each Palace attempt to grow, actually flourishes well here. It is a red and white rose, both colors in one.

August 8, 1544

It was almost exactly one year ago that Edward and Mary and I accompanied Father and Catherine Parr to Woodstock. We all felt so safe and happy at Woodstock. The plague had broken out in London early on in the summer. That was when Father first fled with Edward. He had engaged Catherine Parr as Edward's tutor, and then they simply fell in love. How things change so fast! Catherine began as a tutor and became a Queen. I began as a Princess and have become twice now within one year an exile! But my father is not a cruel man. I refuse to believe that. He is a man of whims and sudden rages, but I know he must love me. He just must.

August 9, 1544

Miracle of miracles — another sunny day, well over a week without rain! I shall go out this afternoon and gather some pennyroyal for my father. He does like his pennyroyal mixed with civet and musk for his bath. It helps his aching joints. I do pray that my father is not wounded as he wages his war in France. But they say it goes well — that he is within striking distance of Boulogne now. That is his goal, to lay siege to the city and teach King Francis I of France a lesson about England's power.

August 10, 1544

I received my third letter from Princess Mary today. She is consumed with the state of my soul and bids me to pray still more. Has she nothing more interesting to do than worry about my soul? It is so odd with Mary. I think in her own strange way she does truly care for me, but she has a strange habit of speaking carelessly and even cruelly. In addition to telling me about the extra s's they had to squeeze in for my birth announcement, she told me that a tournament had been planned to celebrate the birth of a Prince, but Father canceled it when I was born. Why did she have to tell me all that? Something is not right in Mary's head.

Later

Another mean thing that Mary told me: She said that when I was a small child after my mother had been beheaded, that I looked like a street urchin. It was before Kat had come to take care of me, when Lady Margaret Bryan was my nurse. I remember her — Muggie, I called her. Father apparently had not sent money for my clothing for some time, and Muggie had to write and beg him for cloth, for I had outgrown all my clothes.

I have no recollection myself of threadbare smocks and petticoats. I barely remember my mother. I know she was dark. I know that, and that she favored yellow dresses, but my father also favors yellow.

There is one scene that people have talked about so much that I sometimes think I remember it. It was right after my mother had been arrested. We were all at Greenwich Palace, and Mother was about to be sent to the

Tower. They say that she ran across the courtyard with me in her arms and stood before an open window where my father looked down. She held me high up and cried to the King to spare this child's mother. I think sometimes I remember the lifting up, my mother's voice, the King, my father, looking down from his window. I hear the rustle of my mother's yellow gown. I see the gold of my father's doublet. His chest is immense. He appears like a sun rising in the window, but I cannot see his face for the sun in the sky is too bright. There is no face. There is no voice.

My mother's beheading seems misty and not quite real to me, a dark fairy story. Tales do collect about it, fanciful ones. People in the country, where superstition is high, claim that the hares ran down the roads in great packs the instant my mother's head fell from her shoulders. The hare is the sign of the witch, and some say that every May 19, the anniversary of my mother's execution, the hares run wild. But I have never seen even a single hare hopping about on May 19 and I always look, whether I am here at Hatfield or at Greenwich Palace, or Richmond or Woodstock or Elysynge, or any number of the palaces we often visit in May. I do not for one minute believe that my mother was a witch. Not for one second.

August 10, 1544

I must make a list of the good things, the things that really make Hatfield so lovely, and turn my mind from the dark things that did occupy me last night.

1. No need for mulberry branches under the bed, for there are no fleas here. I need not wear my flea patch, either. I hate to have to wear that pad of fur in my clothes during the summer. It is too hot.

2. There is an abundance of bayberry and juniper, the twigs of which when peeled make the best brushing wands for cleaning one's teeth.

3. Hatfield is generally the most vermin-free of all the palaces in which I live through the year. We only have to employ two rat catchers here. At Hampton Court there are upward of thirty, and they spend their entire time doing nothing but catching rats.

4. The floor rushes stay cleaner much longer because there are so few people and no large banquets held.

5. No rabbit pie for breakfast, but the best cider and cheese are made here in Hatfield. I could live on cider and

cheese. Oh, yes, and the cook makes excellent treacle, which Kat and I spread thickly on our morning porridge.

6. There is the river Lea, which Kat and I go to every sunny day with the cook's son, and we catch fish — freshwater mullet and pike and brown trout. We sometimes have fish for breakfast.

7. And finally, although this is not especially an attribute of Hatfield itself, when I am here, no one thinks about marrying me off. Marriage negotiations are a favorite pastime of the court and my father's Privy Council. There is always a French prince or a future king out there that Father is angling after either for Mary or for me. These negotiations have the unique ability to bore while at the same time frighten me. I have seen enough of my father's matrimonial turmoils to understand that marriage for a woman is a risky thing, a dangerous business.

I am ashamed that I have been bored here, despite the lack of marriage negotiations. But if truth be told, if I seek out the deepest shadows within my heart, it is not boredom that afflicts me. It is the overwhelming sense of loneliness. I am so alone, even with Kat, I sometimes feel crushed by the weight of this feeling. I never thought of loneliness as having weight. But it does. And sometimes it is as if I am ambushed by doubts of my father's love. It is there. I know somewhere in that immense hulk of the King there is a part that loves me. There must be.

August 12, 1544

There is no better breakfast than the purple blackberries that grow here at Hatfield, and there they were this morning in my bowl. Big and fat, floating in thick cream. Oh, if they grew all the year round! I would eat them every day and never tire of them. I ate no bread, no cheese, this morning, just bowl after bowl of berries. Kat said I shall be sick. I shant.

August 13, 1544

Glory! I leave for Hampton Court tomorrow to rejoin the Court. The letter came today. The dear Queen wrote my father and he insists I be with the other children. He hopes to be back from France in another six weeks. By then he promises Boulogne will be his! An autumn of victory celebrations. Richard Cox shall be teaching both me and Edward. Then soon it will be Christmas and there will be holiday masking and presents and banquets.

August 20, 1544
Elsynge Palace

We take our time getting to Hampton Court, as Kat insists that we stop at Elsynge Palace on the way, as she claims she has some clothes she has left there that would be required for the chill weather of fall. But I think she has another reason — to see John Ashley, who is here. We have been here two days, hawking and hunting in the magnificent deer park and, in the evening, playing endless games of cards. I played miserably, as I am distracted with thoughts of getting to Hampton Court and seeing Robin and Edward.

August 23, 1544
Hampton Court

Kat insists on many things when we first arrive at a new Palace. We must personally check for rats, and more importantly, we must check for poison. Kat is obsessed with poisonings. She claims the courtiers at Hampton Court are full of wiles and deadly designs. Here everyone seeks status, and they will do anything to displace a rival. Including murder. So she insists on washing off all the fruit in the baskets placed in our apartments and checking all the bedclothes for poisonous dusts. I have even caught her plunging an ox horn into our food and drink. It is supposedly an antidote against poison. I think it is just a silly old superstition, and I cannot understand why a learned lady such as Kat would believe such nonsense.

Poison is the one thing which Kat and I really disagree about. I do not think anyone would ever try to poison me, because I am simply not important enough, and I certainly do not think that running around with an ox horn will do one wit of good. So I set off to see Roger Ponsby, the Revels Master. His workrooms are by Fish Court. I am much more interested in costumes, as Saint Michael's feast is coming up and there shall be a grand masque.

There were several people in the courtyard when I arrived — fishmongers and cooks and cooks' assistants. Two youngsters directly in my path were wrestling with a large basket of fish. Their heads were wrapped in sweating cloths that nearly hid their eyes. I may have been a Princess in exile, but I am back now by my father, King Henry VIII's, command. People must make way and certainly not block my path with a smelly basket of fish. But the bumbling idiots, not looking where they were going, stumbled right into me. I fell. The fish flew. One caught in the lacings of my stomacher band and another in the ruff round my neck. "You will go to the Tower!" I shouted, but suddenly the boys whipped off their sweating cloths and who stood before me but Robin and Edward. They, too, were dripping with dead fish and laughing so hard they could not speak. All my anger vanished, for even with an eel hanging from his neck, Robin looked so good, and dear Edward had an octopus on his shoulder. I hugged them both, and the whole courtyard roared with laughter.

Oh, I know I am back in Court again. There are jests and minstrels and fools and the weight of the loneliness slides away. I am so light I might float.

August 25, 1544

"We must conquer the Captains of Ignorance as your father, the King, now conquers the French. He lays siege to

Boulogne." And with that our tutor, Richard Cox, pulls down the map and shows us the deployments of the thousands of troops that now encircle the French city. We mark with pins the positions of the vanguard, the rear guard, and the King's battle. In the King's battle alone there are thirteen thousand soldiers. Our math problems are feeding problems. We must calculate how much is required to keep the army fed. By decree each soldier is allowed one pound of biscuits, one pound of beef, and one gallon of beer a day.

This is the way to learn. Richard Cox is the most exciting teacher we have ever had. Edward tries to do shortcuts with the mathematics, and he always makes careless mistakes. Master Cox is not afraid to scold the Prince of the realm. But he does it with such good cheer that even Edward does not mind. Our brains, says Master Cox, shall glow like the most majestic of orbs in our skulls lighting the way for the world, for Britannia!! "Rule Britannia!" he squawks at the top of his voice. His thin, sandy-colored hair flies about his skull like pale licks of flame. He is really a most peculiar and wonderful person.

August 26, 1544

The glass fitters, carvers, and plasterers are hard at work still. There is no rest for them in the house of Tudor, as my father changes wives so often. In the stateroom I had noticed that Catherine Howard's initials and personal crest, the crowned Tudor rose, was replaced by Catherine Parr's maiden rising from the Tudor rose. My father was not married to Anne of Cleves long enough for them to paint, carve, or plaster her symbols anywhere. With over thirty Palaces, this is a lot of work for the chief glassmaker and plasterer Galyon Hone. Crest changing is one of my earliest memories. My mother's leopard was transformed into Jane Seymour's panther. And then came Catherine Howard's crowned Tudor rose. Alas, I do not like to think of Catherine Howard. I shall think of something else. It is but twelve days until my birthday.

August 27, 1544

Such fun today. Master Cox suggested we break early from our lessons and go to the tennis courts. Robin and I are quite good, but Edward is so short he barely reaches over the net. So we sent a message through Princess Mary's fool, Lucretia the Tumbler, to fetch her, for Mary is quite good at tennis and would be a good partner for Edward. Robin says never was a fool so wasted as Lucretia on Mary. Fools are supposed to be constantly available to make one's life bright and gay. To tell a joke, recite a naughty ditty, sometimes to do a tumble or somersault. Lucretia has an assistant, so to speak, a woman named Jane the Bald. Very odd indeed is Jane. She wears stylish gowns of damask, but on her feet she wears the shoes of a clown with curled-up toes, and her head she keeps shaved bald as an egg!

We had a good game. Lucretia was scorekeeper.

August 28, 1544

Master Cox spoke to us today about astronomy, my passion, and he told me that there was a Polish man named Copernicus who had a theory that all the planets circle the sun. Master says that my father had studied this theory with his good friend Thomas More. Unfortunately, Thomas More was beheaded by my father because he did not sign the paper that allowed Father to become the supreme leader of the Church of England. Thomas is not a good name to have. My father has beheaded many Thomases: Thomas More, Thomas Cromwell, and very nearly Thomas Wolsey, though he died before the execution.

August 30, 1544

With all this rain, I have had time to find a place to hide you, dear diary. It is an old prayer niche. My apartments were at one time occupied by a lady of Queen Catherine of Aragon's Court. They were all devout Catholics, and Catherine delighted in rewarding them with small relics, which they kept in the prayer niches. This one was all cobwebby. There was an ancient wood panel covering it. I cleaned out the spiders and a mouse's nest. No one will suspect you are in there, diary.

August 30, 1544

Still rains. We are getting very bored and unruly in the schoolroom. Princess Mary passed by and heard Master Cox scolding us. She popped in and suggested we go to Chapel with her for prayer and he actually agreed. We, all three of us, are furious with Master Cox. But we had no choice and had to follow Princess Mary.

September 1, 1544

All this rain and prayer is not only boring but depressing. My thoughts turn dark. Shadows begin to gather like night birds in my mind. They glide across my half dreams in the perpetual darkness of these dreary days. And when I get like this, I begin to hear the crying again, the crying of Catherine Howard. You see Catherine is now a ghost. She never rests, but haunts the Long Gallery of Hampton Court. She often comes with the darkness of my mind, but sooner or later others hear her as well.

September 2, 1544

Robin heard her, too, last night. So now we must do what is required to put her poor spirit at ease so the rest of us can be in peace. The adults pretend they never see her or hear her. But I know they do. In particular, I know my father does. He is the most plagued of all by her ghost. So now I must tell you the dreadful story of Catherine Howard.

It was said that she had been with other men before she had married my father and since, including Thomas Culpeper, a gentleman of my father's Privy Chamber. It is a crime of highest treason to be unfaithful to the King. There was no choice except to arrest her. But Father was still slow in the doing of it and proceeded with great care, as he had loved Catherine. For a while there was some talk of sending her away to a convent.

Many thought my father would never execute her. She was under house arrest first at Hampton Court, and just before she was to be taken to the Tower, she broke loose from the guard and ran screaming down the Long Gallery that leads to the Royal Chapel. She had thought my father was in the Chapel praying. Her screams for mercy could be heard throughout the west wing of Hampton Court. But Father was not there. He was out hunting. Robin and I were there, however. We saw her. It was a sight I shall never forget. Her eyes slid back in her skull until only the whites were visible. She knocked over a statue, which shattered on the marble floor but it did not break her speed. Her hair streamed out behind her, and she frothed. Yes, she actually frothed at the mouth. It was the most ghastly sight I have ever seen. Robin and I clutched each other, and it was then that I whispered in Robin's ear that I should never ever marry.

Catherine was executed on February 13, 1542. Part of me wished I were nowhere near, but we were at Whitehall Palace right in London, a short distance from the Tower. There was, however, another part of me that wished to be near. I felt a bond with her. She was really more of a play-mate than a Queen. She had once given me a small jeweled pendant. I still have it. I think she was just too young to be Queen and certainly to be my father's wife.

Just before the ax fell, she called out, "I die a Queen, but I would rather die the wife of Culpeper."

But perhaps she was neither playmate nor wife, and that is why she haunts us now. The ghost knows not who she is. So Robin has this idea that we must show the ghost its true nature. To this end we sneak out of our chambers just as the guard changes at four in the morning. We take our small ninepins. They are like pegs that stand up. We used to play ninepins with Catherine. Robin says it is our solemn duty to play this game in the Long Gallery. If we do this, it shall ease her spirit, for it is a way of saying to her that we are still her friends despite all. And, in fact, the shrieking does stop. The other odd thing about our forays into the Long Gallery is that we are never caught. It is as if a kindly spirit looks after us. We seem to pass unnoticed by anybody. It is as if we ourselves become wraiths of the night.

September 4, 1544

The ghost is quiet. She screams no more. Robin sent me the signal to meet him last night. He slipped me a ninepin in Vespers just as we knelt. At a quarter before the hour I was out of my bed. I put a cloak over my night rail, the gown I wear for sleeping. Kat snored away. I met him in the Long Gallery, and under the immense hanging tapestry of Diana the goddess of the hunt we played four rounds of ninepins. The night shadows began to slip away and the thin light of the dawn slid through the upper gallery windows. I looked up and for the first time in days realized that the sky was clear, and not only clear, but the morning star shone brightly. "Tomorrow I wager Master Cox will take us to the roof to look through the telescope," I whispered to Robin.

"Too bad Catherine is not here for that. She would have loved viewing the night sky," Robin answered.

"But, Robin, she is the night sky now." And with that I felt the gentlest breeze stir my hair.

September 5, 1544

Oh, I am so shivering cold. I am just back from observing the stars. Master Cox took us all to the rooftop, to the stargazing platform that Father had erected. He brought with him a set of Father's speculative glasses, which his eyeglass maker makes for him. They are a series of lenses by which one can bring distant objects closer if indeed you line them up. So tonight we brought closer Mars, glowing and red. We all gave hurrahs for the warrior star for we thought of Father laying siege to Boulogne. Master Cox reminds us again of the Polish man who said that the sun does not revolve around the earth, but the earth around the sun. If the sun does not revolve around the earth, if the earth is not the center, that means England is not the center of the earth, and if England is not the center, it means my father, King Henry VIII, is not the center of this universe, and this I do believe could upset him. He is, however, at heart a man of science and learning.

September 7, 1544

Today is my birthday and it was a most wonderful one. The Queen herself gave me a lovely and thoughtful gift — a very small book of meditations illustrated with lovely woodcuts. Robin gave me a hawking glove and promises to let me fly his favorite merlin. Edward, the dear child, gave me — well, you shall never guess — a monkey! He said his monkey, Hotspur, needs a friend. So he arranged with the keeper of the Royal Menagerie to procure one for me. We plan to teach them tricks together. I think I shall call my monkey Memo. Memo was one of my father's favorite minstrels, and I think the name suits a monkey, and it might please Father.

September 8, 1544

The Queen absolutely forbids us to play with the monkeys in any of the drawing rooms and Master Cox will not allow them in the school. So we went into the Pond Garden. Memo raced for the water, and we were terribly frightened he might jump in and drown. Then Edward suggested that we go to the tennis courts. I thought this quite brilliant and said perhaps we could teach Memo and Hotspur to play tennis!

September 10, 1544

Memo is improving in lessons. The tennis court is an ideal training ground for we can raise and lower the net and teach him to jump over it. We shall introduce a tennis ball soon and just accustom him to the idea of bouncing it. I have studied Memo's hands carefully. The fingers are extraordinarily long. Holding the ball will not be hard. Holding the tennis racket I think will prove more difficult. Edward is working with Hotspur on perfecting what he calls a good simian grip.

September 14, 1544

Michaelmas is just two weeks away. Edward and I want to masquerade as stars or perhaps entire constellations. We go to Ponsby this afternoon to discuss our costumes for the dance following the Feast of Saint Michael's. Ponsby showed us how he might fix our costumes as constellations. Robin has decided to be Orion. Edward is to be Aquila the eagle. Ponsby shall fashion him some wings. And I shall be Cygnus the swan. My costume in many senses is the easiest, for swan and goose are two favorite dishes to serve for Michaelmas feast. So there shall be several freshly slaughtered swans from which Ponsby can fashion my wings. I think it shall be beautiful.

September 15, 1544

Glorious news. The Queen received today a letter from Father. Boulogne is about to fall. He said it would have fallen sooner but for a shortage of gunpowder. There were considerable details about batteries and mines and bulwarks and dikes, but at the end he said, "Hearty blessings to all of our children." <u>All</u>, dear diary, Father said <u>All</u>! He meant me. <u>Me! Me! Me!</u> I am so excited I am no longer an exile. <u>Me! Me!</u> My father loves <u>Me</u>! I am just a fool. I would be content writing <u>Me</u> all the livelong day. Oh, glory! I cannot wait to see him.

September 19, 1544

The Queen is so busy that we hardly ever see her. She has many jobs as Regent. It is the Queen who must oversee the shipment of supplies to France, and through the Royal Lieutenant of the Privy Council she must keep a careful watch on the rebellious Scots on the northern border. The Scots are allies of the French, and only two weeks ago our vessels captured a Scottish one carrying secret letters to France. Queen Catherine seized the letters and sent them on to Father. She looks so tired. That is why we did not protest when she called us in and said that Lady Jane Grey was coming to court and that we must be nice to her and arrange for a Michaelmas costume through Ponsby, so she won't feel left out.

Lady Jane Grey is a granddaughter of my father's sister. So I guess that makes her my cousin. However, Lady Jane Grey is a simpering idiot as far as I am concerned. Oh, she is bright enough. Very scholarly, almost as good as me in Latin and Greek. Although I doubt she can hold a candle to me now in mathematics. We are now all doing Euclidean geometry with great facility. But Jane Grey is dull, dull, dull. I would wager she will not even care about a costume for the Michaelmas Feast. She is like Princess Mary in that sense. No imagination. Not quite as dour as Mary. Robin said the most curious thing about Mary — that the reason she changes her hair color so much is because she finds it easier than changing the expression on her face. Her mouth is always in a straight firmly pressed line — just like a pleat on my bodice. That tight, that neat, only horizontal instead of vertical.

September 20, 1544

I am being very nice to Lady Jane Grey. She arrived yesterday. Master Cox is already calling her Good Jane or Diligent Jane after only one day in the schoolroom. It's not as if I am bad or stubborn. I find it very annoying to hear him go on in this manner about her. She is so dull. Why doesn't he call her Dull Jane?

September 21, 1544

We took Lady Jane Grey to Ponsby to be fitted up for a costume. The whole way there she was going on about how sweet it was, that we shouldn't take the time, and so forth and so on. Then when we get there she is so overwhelmed with all the fantastical devices and costumes that she cannot make up her mind what she wants to be. She hems and haws. "Oh, I think I shall be this. Oh, I think I shall be that. I think I should be something from the Bible." The desert that Moses wandered through for forty years is what I think — dry, blank, and featureless. Finally I cannot stand it another minute. I make up her mind for her. "Pegasus," I say. "You will be the constellation Pegasus." Well, the poor girl weeps for joy. "Oh, dear Elizabeth. You are so kind. So imaginative. I would never have thought of this myself. Oh, a winged horse!" She does an awkward little dance around Ponsby's workshop and nearly whinnies! This girl is going to drive me mad! And needless to say, our heavens shall be a little less lustrous with the constellation of Lady Jane Grey. Grey! How appropriate that is her last name. It suits.

September 22, 1544

Sometimes I simply cannot fathom Mary. She invited me and Lady Jane Grey to play cards with her and Lucretia the Tumbler and Jane the Bald in her apartments this afternoon. She plays not just ruthlessly but with such snide remarks, especially to me. Lady Jane Grey had begun to explain about our Michaelmas costumes. I must give her credit — she praises me mightily, saying how clever I am. Saying Princess Elizabeth did this and Princess Elizabeth planned that.

Now you must understand that Mary has never called me Princess to my face, and I can tell that all this is grating on her a bit. (I have no qualms about addressing her as Princess.) Suddenly she turns to me and says in that low voice of hers, which seems quite startling coming out of her heart-shaped face, "Let me see, Sister, so Robin is going as Orion and Prince Edward as an eagle and Lady Jane as Pegasus. Why do you not go as a hare?" There is dead silence at the card table.

Everyone knows that hares are the symbols of witches. This is a direct assault on my mother, whom she still does hate with a passion, for it was for my mother that Father left her mother, Catherine of Aragon. I appear to concentrate very hard on my cards, but I look up slowly and directly into her bitter gray eyes and say in an even voice,

"We are going as constellations, Princess Mary. To the best of my knowledge there is no starry configuration that resembles a hare."

"But what," persisted Mary, "is the animal that Orion slays and holds in his hand?" I cannot believe the words I am hearing, but at this very moment Jane the Bald recovers her wits, thank God, and she begins juggling with the apples from a bowl while reciting a bawdy limerick. Jane must have been desperate to recite such a limerick in front of Lady Jane Grey and me. Oh, well, it very much saved the day. Why does Mary dislike me so? Though, I must admit, there are times she is pleasant to me.

Later That Evening

Did I say "save the day"? Or so I thought. Lady Jane Grey came to my apartments an hour ago to offer me her support. Indeed, she was livid. I was overwhelmed by her emotion and suddenly I found myself rather drawn to Jane Grey. She told me that Princess Mary said something extremely horrible. I sensed immediately it must be about my mother's beheading. So to set her at ease I said, "If it is about my mother's beheading, do not worry." I wanted to know what Mary had been saying.

"Well," Jane Grey said in a low trembly voice, "Mary said that at the moment Anne Boleyn's head fell from her neck, the tapers around her own mother's tomb at Peterborough House spontaneously lit themselves."

I howled at that one, simply howled with laughter. And when Lady Jane saw how hard I laughed, she seemed relieved.

Still Later

Quite a parade in here tonight. My next visitor who just left minutes ago was Jane the Bald. Here, in summary, is what she spilled out in her breathless way: "Lucretia said I must come to you, dear child. You know she (meaning Princess Mary) is simply not right in the head."

What did I tell you, diary? Jane leans forward and the light from my tapers reflects off her shiny bald head. "You see, dear, when you were born, Princess Mary was first stripped of her title of Princess. Your father decided there should only be one Princess and it was to be you. She would be simply Lady Mary. Your father wanted his marriage to her mother to be considered invalid. And then, besides all that, your mother, Anne Boleyn, insisted that Mary go live with you at Hatfield as a sort of menial servant in your nursery. The King and Queen were not there often, but when they were, Anne was very nasty to Mary. She even encouraged her Ladies-in-Waiting to slap her and abuse her with words."

"But did not my father interfere?"

"I do not think he saw it, dear. She was careful not to do it around him." At this point Jane took my hand in hers and squeezed it with great sympathy. "But your father was simply blind to Anne Boleyn's faults in the beginning. He was transfixed by her."

"Do you believe my mother was a witch?" Dread swirled in my stomach.

"No, dear. I believe that it was the same as with Princess Mary — something was very wrong in your mother's head."

Jane the Bald left twenty minutes ago. I shall not sleep well tonight. If my mother was not a witch, she was insane. And so is Princess Mary. Does that mean I, too, shall be insane? This is not a very good heritage, nor much of a choice: to be crazy or a witch.

September 23, 1544

I am so irritated with Kat. She insists that we bathe today. Bathing wrecks a perfectly good day. It takes so long — all morning the servitors bring up steaming vats of water to pour into the tubs. It takes forever to fill them. I cannot understand why we have to do this. We just had baths barely three weeks ago! And, of course, before we bathe and do the hair washing, we must comb through our hair for nits. I say, why not just drown the stupid bugs? Why spend all this time before we wash our hair chasing them down? I mean, it is not fun like hunting. Hardly a blood sport, picking a nit. No real skill involved as with the crossbow.

September 24, 1544

Woke up with a terrible headache and stomach cramps. It is probably from having to take a bath. Kat wants to give me a glyster. A glyster is an awful treatment where water is pumped into one's bowels. It is supposed to relieve them of pain. It causes pain! And one spends the entire day or night sitting on the pot. If I were Queen, I would outlaw glysters.

September 25, 1544

Still sick. Dr. Butts came to visit me, but he is so old himself and short of wind I thought he might keel over before he got to my bedside. I do hope I recover in time for Michaelmas. Lady Jane and Robin came to visit me today. It is forbidden that Edward visit me, as he is not allowed near anyone who is sick. I should be thankful for this rule because, if Edward dies, Mary becomes Queen, and I might as well die if that is the case.

September 26, 1544

I have three days to get well. I am determined to. They gave me pennyroyal mixed with watered wine for my sore throat, but it did not sit well in my stomach. In fact, it danced. Queen Catherine has sent an herbal mixture sewn into a bag that is supposed to be steeped in tea and put on my forehead for my headaches. She has also sent many fresh flowers. There is nothing nicer than fresh flowers in the sick chamber. Catherine herself always has her apartments brimming daily with fresh flowers. She keeps lovely apartments, and her greyhounds are so well trained she permits them in her drawing rooms. I wish I had dogs to fill up my apartments here. My chamber is too large. I feel like a pea rattling around in it.

September 27, 1544

Had cheese and bread and watered ale for dinner last night and porridge for breakfast and kept it all down. I shall be well for Michaelmas! I just know it.

September 28, 1544

I am well but Kat will let me do nothing. I am so bored. She insists that I stay in bed. She says it is very easy to relapse. I say I shall collapse if I do not practice getting up. She says that perhaps this afternoon she will allow me to go with the children to Ponsby's workshop to try on our costumes. I forgot to mention that during my illness, word came that Father's assault on Boulogne has been successful. The city surrendered and we hear that on September 18 Father rode triumphantly through the gates of Boulogne. But with all this glory there is one very dark cloud. Kat now tells me that they feared mightily that during my sickness it was not some simple complaint but indeed plague! So that is why not even Robin and Lady Jane came to visit but once. For indeed plague now rages in all the channel ports and in London. And it was not just a plague but the sweating sickness, and is the most dreadful of all diseases imaginable. It strikes suddenly and it is said that people's blood boils with the high fever. Great swellings the size of oranges grow in their armpits, and one's head aches as if cleft with an ax! Death is usually within a few short hours.

Right now it is said that nearly one out of every four houses in every port city has the sweating sickness. The Queen has been beset with worry, for how might the King return to his realm if every entry to England is barricaded by the festering plague? She and the Privy Council have been meeting for long hours to map out a route that will be the safest for Father to return to England.

September 30, 1544

There was never such a Michaelmas celebration, as everyone was nearly drunk with joy over the fall of Boulogne. There were thirty-three courses. Naturally there was goose, which is traditional. Over five hundred were roasted, along with two dozen swans, one of whose wings I wore. There was also rabbit, lamb, quail, and lamprey eel (one of Father's favorites even though he was not here). For the sweets what I like best, snow pudding. But most spectacular was a sugar replica of *Great Harry*, Father's flagship, with dozens of tiny sailors molded from almond paste.

There was a performance, a mummery, in which an immense construction in the form of Mount Olympus was wheeled to the center of the Great Hall. It had real trees growing from it and was spilling with ivy and all sorts of flowers. On top was a figure of Zeus and his Queen, Hera, and Court ladies and gentlemen dressed as the gods. There were several wild and vulgar centaurs — men naked to the waist and wearing pointed ears and breeches made from animal skins with tails attached. They galloped round the hall and tried to kiss the ladies. The ladies pretended not to like it and screamed, but I think they did like it. I could tell. It made me wonder what a kiss might be like. Like candy? Like treacle on porridge? Sweet but not too sweet. I do wonder.

Soon it was time for us to appear. Ponsby had made a rolling platform draped in midnight blue velvet that rose behind us. He had with much skill suspended swing seats on which we were perched and could swing against the drapery of the "sky." A hush fell upon everyone as we were rolled in. Robin wore a glittering jerkin over a white tunic. The skin of the rabbit he carried had been drenched in silver dust. Lady Jane Grey, as Pegasus the winged horse, was completely clad in a suit of sparkling silver. On her head she wore a silky mane of silver tassels. Ponsby had fashioned Edward's eagle wings from turkey feathers. Then he had made for Edward a helmet with a gilt beak. And as Cygnus I wore the third pair of wings. I had perfected the wafting movements. Not a bit of my red hair showed under the headdress, and around my eyes was painted a design of silver and gold.

I shall never forget this Michaelmas.

October 1, 1544

Father returned today. He is much renewed by the campaign in France. He is much thinner. His color good. His step lively. He was most anxious to see the royal children and we were called for immediately. We all had so much to tell him that we had to take turns speaking. Well, Princess Mary did not say so much. She, I could tell, was hoping that Father might have some news for her about a husband.

The daughters of Kings are indeed like pawns on a chessboard and stand ready to be offered in marriage to secure new allies against an enemy. Father has been searching most diligently for a husband for Mary for many years. For a time there was talk of Mary and the Duke of Orleans. Then there was talk of a relative of Anne of Cleves as a possible husband.

When I was not even a year old, Father proposed a marriage between me and the third son of the King of France. The actual betrothal would not have taken place until I was seven. Then we would live apart until I was fourteen. That, however, fell through some years ago. But as I have said, I shall never marry. And certainly never if I were

Queen. Why, if one were Queen, would one ever want to marry? If one is ruler, is it not better to be both King and Queen? That is exactly what a woman can do if she remains without a mate.

October 3, 1544

Edward and I gave a demonstration of our monkeys' talents on the tennis courts. Father roared with laughter. He proposed that we play what he called Varied Triples. He and I and Memo against Catherine, Edward, and Hotspur. It was so much fun. I think Memo is an exceptionally bright little monkey. I am forever grateful to Edward for giving him to me. In less than two weeks it will be Edward's birthday, and I am at a loss as to what to give him. In addition, I must also think of a fitting Christmas gift for the Queen, for truly she was the one who brought me back from exile, I am sure, with her words to Father. The autumn months fly by so quickly. I wonder where we shall celebrate Christmas this year.

October 5, 1544

The Palace is really beginning to stink. Hampton Court is the worst for this. Everyone goes about with their noses buried in pomander balls to hide the stench. Part of the problem is that the population of the Court has nearly doubled since Father's return. More food is being served; therefore, there is more garbage and more spills on the rushes that cover the floors. There is a stink of sour wine everywhere because some of these courtiers bring large retinues of servants who swill away great quantities, and in their drunkenness spill some or sometimes vomit. Even though the stools on which we sit in our privies are covered with velvet and satin, the air is terrible. Kat orders fresh flowers strewn everywhere, and I wear a nosegay pinned to my kirtle.

Most likely when we leave we shall go either to Westminster or to Whitehall Palace.

October 6, 1544

It is Whitehall for Christmas. We leave in two days. And that is none to soon. When Kat and I returned to our apartments this evening, we found a huge fat rat sitting on Kat's embroidery hoop!

The chamberlains of the wardrobes have already left with many of the clothing trunks and personal items. Furniture of course need not be moved. Our apartments are fitted with our favorite things. Master Holbein knew that we children adored his pencil-and-charcoal sketches of animals. So we all have lovely drawings of animals in our chambers in all the Palaces.

October 7, 1544

I have settled upon a present for Edward. And none too soon, for there is precious little time to prepare it. I must translate as quickly as possible a few of Aesop's *Fables* from the Greek into the English. Master Cox is about to start Edward on the fables. I think I, too, started the translations when I was about seven.

October 10, 1544
Whitehall Palace

We are installed in Whitehall now. Kat took forever settling us in. Her fear of poison! She mutters that the Palace is so old it would be hard to tell the poison from the dust. In spite of Whitehall's being rather shabby, I do prefer it to Greenwich or Hampton Court. The bedchambers are smaller here and the windows bigger. In fact, the windows in my chamber have window seats, which I stack with cushions and pillows. It makes a cozy place to read, and I can see the river and all the barges progressing up and down it. In my bed at night, I never let the servitors draw the curtains around it. I leave them wide open so I can see out the windows. At night, from my bed, the river can be lovely. The torches that light the barges reflect on the water, and on damp, cool mornings the mist hovers over the river like a cloud, and the riverboats and barges seem to float in the air.

Father is in a very foul mood so we are careful not to go anywhere near him. He is furious because Charles V, King of Spain and Holy Roman Emperor of the German states, has made a separate peace with France. Charles was our ally, and he never even consulted with Father's envoys. Charles had once been thought of a possible match for Princess Mary. No more!

October 11, 1544

We were required in the King's audience chambers yesterday. I was generally invisible, as Father was most focused on Edward and Mary. He did not look well. When he entered the room, we children were all shocked at the change in him. He required a stave under each arm to walk. His bulk has increased noticeably since his return. Two attendants were needed to help him into his chair. I noticed that his legs were bandaged under his hose, and by the end of the audience a stain had appeared on his calf, which means the leg sores are festering again. They come and they go, these leg sores. Mostly come of late. Dr. Butts says they are caused by poor and sluggish movement of the blood. The Queen appeared pale and tense, and even Will Somers, Father's fool, looked strained. But he did say something toward the end to make Father grin. Will depends on language alone for fool's work. There are no somersaults or tricks. He wears no bells or curled toe shoes. He is all wit.

October 12, 1544

Edward's birthday. There was a grand feast. Father seemed much merrier. Jane the Bald and Lucretia the Tumbler did a very funny play based on Aesop's *Fables* in which they wore various animal heads and cavorted around the Great Hall. Master Cox must have told everyone that Edward is studying Aesop's *Fables*, for the royal baker wheeled out a table of custards and puddings all sculpted into the shapes of animals from the tales. But for me, the best part of the evening was when Father called me to his place and said, "Dear child, I saw your gift to the Prince. It is an eloquent and witty translation." Then he gave my cheek a squeeze. I looked down and blushed a bit. Then I saw his leg. It was leaking again. Poor Father. Aaah, but I can almost still feel the pinch he gave my cheek. It is lovely. I wish it had turned red and left a mark.

October 14, 1544

Whitehall Palace is a strange place. They say that it was one of the most splendid Palaces ever built. There were blooming gardens and magnificent tapestries. The woodwork was the finest. But now the tapestries hang dusty and moth-eaten. The gilt on all the moldings is tarnished and chipped. The gardens and the tiltyard, where they once had tournaments, are choked with weeds. Lady Jane Grey, however, had the best idea. She feels that a corner of the rose garden might be saved. It has a very sunny exposure, and we might be able to coax it to bloom some Saint Martin's roses. That is what late-blooming roses are called. Saint Martin's Day is November 11.

Because this Palace is in such disrepair, it is quite easy for me to find a hiding place for you, diary. One fireplace in my chamber does not work at all. Loose stones in the flue, so I found a perfect spot for you. One must always wear that dreadful little patch of wool to protect from fleas here at Whitehall, or one would be consumed whole by the little beasts.

October 15, 1544

Jane the Bald came and begged Lady Jane and me to come play cards with Princess Mary and Lucretia. She says that Princess Mary is in a very foul mood because she was still hoping for a marriage with Charles V. Why she would want him I wouldn't know. I heard that he is a man with a huge ugly jaw, bad teeth, and poor digestion. I am sure his breath stinks. Then Jane told me that Mary would have even settled for his son Philip, who will become King of Spain. But Philip is eleven years younger. If I were to take a husband eleven years younger, it would mean I should marry an infant! He might not even know how to crawl yet! I start giggling, for I think that this would make for a ludicrous sight. I start to imagine our wedding, or perhaps a coronation — baby being carried down the nave of Westminster Abbey with ermine-trimmed robes trailing behind. I shall never be Queen and I shall never marry, so none of this is of any consequence. I agree to play cards with Princess Mary if she agrees not to say anything nasty and not cheat.

"Cheat?" says Jane the Bald, her eyebrows sliding up into her glistening scalp in disbelief. I roll my own eyes heavenward and sigh deeply. "Let us not pretend to be fools even though that is your occupation, dear Jane. You and I both know that Princess Mary cheats at cards." Am I to remind Jane that I have had five mothers, two of them were beheaded, one a near girl? I mean, Jane dear, I want to say, if one has half a brain one cannot remain an innocent long in my father's court. Yes, Princess Mary does cheat at cards. And the only reason I agree to go play is because I truly like Lucretia and Jane and feel they need my company much more than Mary does.

Later

Mary was extremely nice to me. So nice it made me nervous. She did cheat once. It was a small point. But I know Jane Grey saw her because she nudged my foot under the table.

October 16, 1544

Queen Catherine talked to us today about a new tutor she might employ, as Master Cox has to go away for a while. We shall miss him terribly. The new tutor's name is John

Cheke. He is a renowned scholar and will give us more advanced work. He probably will not come until the new year. In the meantime, the Queen says we must work very hard on our Greek and Latin so we can rise to the challenges she is sure Master Cheke will give us.

October 17, 1544

Galyon Hone has arrived to begin changing the crests here at Whitehall Palace to Catherine Parr's symbols. There is so much else that needs attention, however. Robin and Lady Jane and Edward and I began our work in the garden this afternoon as it was such a fine day. It is so overgrown with brambles that it seems impenetrable. And we were terribly scratched. Edward gave up immediately and went to sit in the shade and read.

October 18, 1544

Robin is possessed about the garden. We wear hawking gloves to protect our arms, and Robin whacks at the thorny brambles with a gutting knife. He managed to get some shearers from one of the groundsmen for Lady Jane and me. Edward could use his boy's sword, which he received when he turned six. It would be perfect, but instead he sits in the shade and translates Aesop! Sometimes Edward shows a distinct lack of spirit. Now that I think of it, I believe his humors are out of order. There are four fluids in the body which are the four <u>humors</u>: choler (or yellow bile), blood, phlegm, and melancholy (or black bile). If you have too much of one, it is not good. It is thought that there are tests of one's urine that can show such imbalances. I think he should send a sample of his urine to Dr. Butts.

October 20, 1544

Oh, you shall never guess what happened today. Father was taking a walk with Archbishop Cranmer, one of his closest advisers. They took us quite by surprise in the rose garden. Father was so pleased — at least at first, until he spotted Edward languishing in a corner with a book. Then his pleasure turned to outrage. "Look at your sister and Robin and little Lady Jane Grey. They are scratched and bloody from battling thorny roses, sweating and brimming with vigor, and you, you lad, the future King, sit like an overfed milksop. Are you the son of a King who just commanded the largest invasionary force in the history of England and the continent?"

Oh, poor Edward, I really did feel sorry for him. I ran up to Father and curtsied very deeply. "Father," I said in a very small voice, "do not blame Edward. I believe his humors are out of balance." Father leaned over and cupped his hand round my chin and raised me up. "What is this you say, child?" I took a deep breath and did not blush when I said, "I would beseech you to ask Doctor Butts to collect a sample of his urine for study." I almost dared not look up. But then I saw there was nothing but loving kindness in his eyes, a softness almost like the early morning mist. I knew now that he did not look at me as a half witch at all. Indeed, I believe, he had no thoughts of my mother. It was just I, Elizabeth, who filled his eyes and his mind. "Elizabeth, dear child" — he took his thumb and ran it across my cheek — "you are bleeding from the roses." Then he spoke a few short words in Latin — "*Tu eres rosa Tudoris veritas*," which means, "You are the true Tudor rose." This might be the happiest day of my life. I feel as if I have been anointed.

October 21, 1544

Robin came running up to our apartments today brimming with excitement. The best news! When Father saw us battling the thorny roses with our hawking gloves, he ordered that we are to skip lessons this morning and be taken immediately to his armorer at the Tower for better protective covering. So we must rush now, as a barge is coming to convey us from Whitehall Palace down the Thames to the Tower. It is not a long trip. I cannot write anymore now. Must hurry. Kat looks stunned. "Why would children need armor?" she keeps muttering.

October 22, 1544

We worked all afternoon in the garden. We got frightfully hot and finally took off the hauberks and just wore our mail vests, which were much cooler. Edward seems more enthusiastic now that he gets to wear armor.

October 24, 1544

Edward is a tyrant! He refuses to let us touch the roses in the northeast corner, not even to weed them. He claims that these are the ones that his mother, Jane Seymour, planted and that only he can tend them. But he's making a miserable job of it. He and Robin had a huge row. Lady Jane and I just ignored it all and went off and did what we could elsewhere. Sometimes I think it is better to be quiet and just go about one's business.

Later

Hah! I cannot believe I wrote that last sentence. Edward came over and started scolding me and Jane, particularly Jane. I thought she might cry. I got so mad I swore a round and bloody oath that really just about felled everyone in earshot. Robin was astounded. His face shone with admiration. They did not know I knew this sort of language, but I do. I learned it in the Fish Court at Hampton Court. There is a fishmonger who comes there who has a tongue hot as the flames of hell. You cannot use these oaths too often or they wear out, lose their power. That is why I dole them out in very small measure. But my goodness, it works. Edward is as meek as can be.

October 25, 1544

Feeling a bit sad today. No particular reason. Raining. I cannot go out to garden and I am having a bit of trouble with my Greek translation.

Later

You know, dear diary, I must confess, I have lied to you. Something I vowed in my heart I would never do. Earlier I wrote that I did not know why I was sad. I tried to blame it on the weather and then on my Greek translations, but that is not the truth. The truth is something that happened at the Tower that day when we went to get our armor fitted. And now I write here the absolute truth.

I was the first to be measured for my hauberk, and so I asked permission if I could wander off a bit while the others were measured. Master Hawkins said yes, of course, and that I might go in the company of one of the Tower guards. Yeoman Southey was my attendant. "Where would you like to go, My Lady?" he asked.

Now I cannot account for what I said next. The idea just seemed to pop into my head. "Tower Green," I said. His eyes opened wide and his mouth parted in disbelief. You see, dear diary, this was the place where my mother was executed, as well as Catherine Howard. I knew right away I must go there. It was for my mother more than Catherine that I wanted to. I looked him steady in the eye and a round oath bloomed in my head, but never needed to reach my lips. The yeoman simply nodded and took me to Tower Green.

So there I stood on the same ground that held my mother's blood. There was a scaffolding erected and a new block, for indeed they use a fresh block for each execution. They must have been readying for a new beheading, most likely a distinguished person, one who perhaps, like Thomas More, had refused to acknowledge my father as the head of the church. Common criminals are executed on Tower Hill, and throngs of people attend.

I studied the block. There was a curved indentation for the chin to rest on, and then a span of five inches or so for the neck to stretch across. The block was surrounded by straw to soak up the blood. I could feel Yeoman Southey watching me. I turned to him. "Were you here then," I asked, "when they beheaded my mother?" He nodded. "You must then answer every single question I put to you as best you can." He nodded again and said, "As best I can, My Lady."

So now, from what he told me, I know it all. I can picture it precisely. My mother approached the scaffolding from the southeast side. She wore an ermine-trimmed mantle over a dark gray gown also trimmed in fur, and beneath the gown was a scarlet petticoat. The neckline of the gown was purposely low so as not to impede the executioner in his work. She was accompanied by two Ladies-in-Waiting. "Possibly three," the yeoman said. He could not remember. He did remember two ladies helping to remove the headdress, but leaving the coif to hold her hair up from her neck. She knelt down, and her last words were, "To Jesus Christ I commend my soul." And then — this is the hard part for me to write, but I must and I shall do it with a steady hand. The swordsman, in order to get her head in the right position, spoke to a nearby assistant and said, "Bring me the sword." Mother turned her head in the direction he spoke. But he already had the sword concealed at his side, and he quickly raised it and brought it down. In a single stroke my mother's head was cut off. It rolled onto the straw. The cannon boomed.

"Is it true . . ." I began to ask, and then hesitated.

"Is what true?" the yeoman responded.

"Is it true that the eyes in the head still move afterward?"

"Sometimes," the yeoman replied.

"Did my mother's eyes still move?"

"I . . . I . . . I . . ." he began three times, and then finally said, "I don't know."

They did move. His hesitation in answering proved it to me. He wanted to spare me. But I was not for the sparing. I still wanted to know more. If he would not tell me, I am clever and can read between the utterances and the hesitations. But the remainder of the information was forthcoming. My mother's Ladies-in-Waiting covered her head with a white cloth. She was then buried in the Chapel of Saint Peter ad Vincula. Catherine Howard is also buried there. I insisted on being taken to the Chapel. We went and along the way I plucked what few flowers I found growing in the sparsely planted beds that border the walks. I stood first at my mother's grave and then at Catherine's and seeing as I had no vase or water, I merely plucked the petals from the flowers and scattered them atop the graves.

I wrote all this down tonight because I thought it might help. You see, diary, ever since that day I have had the worst nightmares. I hope tonight I shall sleep more peacefully since I have laid down these horrors on your pages.

October 26, 1544

I did sleep better, and today was a lovely sunny day. Master Cox says I make fine progress with my Greek translation. The garden looks so much better, and now that we have cleared it out, we can see that there are many fat rosebuds of the late-blooming variety ready to burst.

October 27, 1544

Played cards with Princess Mary, Jane the Bald, and Lucretia today. I was very, very clever at cards and took several pence from all of them. I could tell that Princess Mary was furious and could barely contain herself, but

Jane kept giving her severe looks. Such looks are especially severe when they come from a gleaming bald head. You can see her scalp flush red, and her eyebrows dart down in a steep plunge like hawks diving for prey.

October 28, 1544

I am nearly too stunned to write. Remember how yesterday I wrote that Princess Mary was so furious at me for winning at cards that she could barely contain herself? Well, she did not. Her meanness spilled over today. Indeed as she spoke to me there was a gleam in her eyes I had not seen before. It seems that Mary somehow found out about my visit to Tower Green. Mary has spies. Everyone knows it. They are mostly Spanish. For her mother, Catherine of Aragon, was Spanish. There are those who still plot to somehow put Mary on the throne. In any case, she approached me after the minstrels played tonight, following dinner in the Great Hall. She led me off into a corner and very slyly said, "I understand that you made a visit to Tower Green." I nodded yes, thinking that something dreadful is to come. "And then to the Chapel where your dear mother is buried." I nodded yes again. "Did Yeoman

Warder Southey tell you perchance that the King had never, if by oversight or intention, ordered a coffin for your dear mother? An old chest was used. It was too short for a normal body. She only fit in it because they could put her head on top of her stomach."

Mary then turned and left. I was left standing there, trembling violently. Lady Jane Grey came up at that instant. "What did she say? What did that frightful old thing say to you, Elizabeth? You are as white as a sheet." I bit my lip so hard I could feel the skin break. I would not speak a word and then suddenly everything tilted and the stone floor came up to meet me. It seems I fainted. Sir Anthony Denny, a groom of the Privy Chamber, rushed over and picked me up and carried me to my apartments. Father was most worried. As a matter of fact, that is to be my revenge. He followed Sir Anthony all the way, and his legs cause him great pain. He insisted that Dr. Butts attend me. Father has just left and I await Dr. Butts. I did not say a word to Father, although he inquired as to what caused me to faint. I hear Dr. Butts now outside my door. Must stop writing.

October 29, 1544

Ah! My revenge is sweet. Although Dr. Butts has prescribed a most loathsome tonic that I must drink twice a
day, a vile concoction of herbs and hyssop leaves mixed
with pennyroyal, Princess Mary is terrified. I am told by
Kat that she paced outside my chamber the entire time
Father was here. Kat said that Princess Mary seemed un-
duly agitated and tried to seek a word with Father, but he
shook her off. She is frightened I told him something.
Fine! Also, no one forces me to eat rabbit pie for breakfast.
I get porridge with extra treacle. There are many benefits
to my position right now.

Later

Oh, I have that woman just where I want her. She sent her
own minstrel today to play for me, as well as a large bou-
quet of flowers. Dr. Butts insists that I stay inside and rest
in my chamber all day. This is fine as long as my bed curtains are not drawn and I get to watch the traffic on the
river. Kat sits in my window seat and reads to me from an
Italian book of verse. Being a little bit sick for a short time

is not so bad. I, of course, am not even a little bit sick. I must just pretend a slight weakness after fainting.

October 30, 1544

All Saints' Day has crept upon us unnoticed. The Queen informs us that Father plans a great celebration on the night before, All Hallows' Eve — tomorrow night. There shall be mummery and apple ducking. The Queen asks that we make lists of our favorite games and entertainments. Here is my list in order of preference:

1. Fireworks
2. Bonfires
3. Chase the Pig

October 31, 1544

Robin, Edward, and Lady Jane Grey and I all put fireworks at the top of our list. I was the only one who wrote down Chase the Pig. It is a rustic game from the country and I see the children around Hatfield playing it all the time. I have longed to play but never have. They find a piglet with the shortest possible tail and the pig is covered with soap. Then it is turned loose to run about through the people, and everyone chases it and tries to catch it by its slippery tail. You have to catch it with one hand and hold it by the tail without touching any other part of the pig. It looks like so much fun. There will definitely be bonfires. We see the stable grooms and other servitors heaping great mounds of wood for the bonfires in the tilt-yard. We also see them nailing hazel branches to all the doors. That should be enough to keep the witches and spirits away.

November 2, 1544

The bonfires still smolder and the servitors are busy taking down the hazel branches. The best part of the entire celebration was Chase the Pig. I came within a hairbreath of catching it. I ripped my dress, got splattered in mud and horse dung. I've never had so much fun in my life. For Lady Jane Grey, of course, it was not exactly Chase the Pig. It was more promenade after the pig. She stepped in one mud puddle, got her slipper wet, and turned white. You would have thought she'd been rammed with a lance in a jousting match. After pig chasing, we ducked for apples. Jane the Bald painted her scalp red and pretended she was one of the apples. She would dunk her head into the cistern along with the apples, and we would nip at it, all in play, of course.

I think I ate too much eel at dinner. By the time they served the swan I could hardly eat a bite. And there was pudding made from the swan's neck. This is Edward's favorite. He ate an enormous amount. There was a sugar replica of Whitehall Palace. Jane the Bald said the funniest thing. She said she wished she could live in the sugar confection as it was in better condition than the Palace. My favorite sweet, however, were the apple fritters. I did manage to eat one. Edward ate twelve!

Princess Mary is still being exceedingly nice to me. I do not know when to trust her. I never shall. But I am enjoying her present fear immensely.

November 3, 1544
Whitehall Palace

Cook sent up leftover apple fritters for my breakfast this morning. She knows how I love them. They were still good. I put a slice of hard cheese on top. When Kat wasn't looking, I tucked one into my sleeve for a snack later in the schoolroom.

November 5, 1544

Master Cox is demanding much of us, as shortly after Saint Martin's Day Edward and I are to be sent to Ashridge House. It is a favorite country mansion for all of us children. We shall be there at least until the Christmas season begins. At Ashridge the new tutors shall join us. So he wants them to be impressed with our progress. Edward is galloping through Aesop's *Fables*. His translations are accurate but lack style to my mind. However, he is just seven. I am not sure if Robin and Lady Jane will accompany us. Princess Mary is to go to Beaulieu, her own Palace in Essex.

November 7, 1544

Our first rose bloomed today and there are others about to burst. It is a true Saint Martin's summer these past few days — warm, sunny, and dry. Everything is bathed in a tawny glow light.

November 8, 1544

Memo tried to eat the second rose! He almost succeeded, but I raced over and gave him a swat and swore a hot and vile oath. He stopped all right, but my timing was most unfortunate, for Father was just coming round the hedge with some of his grooms of the Privy Chamber and the Archbishop of Canterbury. I was simply mortified.

"Was that you, Elizabeth?" I dropped to my knees immediately. I was trembling with fear. Everything had gone so well. What if I were to be exiled again? I could not bear it. I began to speak, still kneeling. "I humbly beseech, Your Majesty. I humbly crave that you will forgive my vile tongue." I heard him turn to someone and say, "She admits her vile tongue." There was the hint of a bemusement in his voice. That could signify either good or bad. One never knows with my father.

Then I heard the fool Will Somers speak: "'Tis not the serpent's forked tongue that speaks with such honesty, Sire."

"Nay," said my father slowly. He was resting his immense weight on the two staves that supported him on his festering legs. I could see the stains on his hose. I could see the ends of the staves sink into the ground on which I knelt. I was too frightened to look up. Will spoke, "Her tongue doth swear, Hal, but her heart in its honesty is true." My father merely grunted at this. Will continued, "Beware the candied tongue, Hal, that laps on royal boots and through its sugary slime conceals the black heart."

A great shadow began to slide across me. It was as if a solar eclipse were occurring. I saw the staves wobble. His great hand came down and cupped my chin and lifted me. "Elizabeth" — he spoke my name coldly — "look at me, girl." When I did, he seemed to gaze upon me with that studied regard as if he were thinking me half witch. He dropped his hand and began to move off with his gentlemen. I did not know the meaning of this. I still don't. I might be banished yet again. I must wait patiently.

November 10, 1544

I have been living with this constant fear of exile now for two days. So far I have heard nothing. Plans seem to proceed as normal for our move to Ashridge. This palace, too, is becoming quite filthy, what with all the banqueting and people and gaming between Michaelmas Feast and the feast of All Saints' Day. The roses bloom in our garden with such vigor, but the stench from the courtyard over the wall outside the kitchens is unbearable.

Kat is mumbling something about baths again. The woman is becoming a fanatic. I think we have had half a dozen baths since summer, and that does not include when we went wading in the river at Hatfield. I say why bother to bathe here at Whitehall when everything and everyone stinks? No one will know the difference. Kat's argument is that we should arrive clean at Ashridge House. Aside from that, I do not wear a wig. That helps me keep my head a lot cleaner because there has been quite a bit of wig bugs. One of Queen Catherine's Ladies-in-Waiting, Lady Dinsmore, who is considered quite beautiful by some (not me), had one crawl out of her wig at dinner. It fell right into that little crack between the breasts that large-breasted ladies love to show. My father said something very bawdy, and everyone screamed with laughter, but I didn't understand the joke. Lady Dinsmore was in such a state that she practically fell into her plate in trying to pick out the bug. So I'm glad I do not wear a wig and I am glad I do not have such large bosoms. And if I did, I would not display them thusly for bugs or anyone else.

November 11, 1544

This is Saint Martin's Day. No lessons. The day celebrates Saint Martin of Tours, who over one thousand years ago saw a beggar freezing and hungry in the streets. He took off his coat and tore it in half, wrapping the beggar in the other half. That night as he slept, in a dream he saw our Lord Jesus wrapped in the very same coat he had torn in half. "Martin," said Jesus, "you have torn your own cloak and wrapped me in it, covering me from the cold."

I like this holiday because for once a saint is not put on a spit or, like Saint Clement, thrown into the sea tied to an anchor, or Saint Catherine, whose body was torn apart on a spiked wheel. The grotesque methods used to kill saints are too many to number.

We went to Matins and, as one might imagine, there was Princess Mary, wrapped in a shredded cloak, kneeling and rocking back and forth, her eyes streaming tears. They say that her mother, Catherine of Aragon, wore a coarse habit under her dresses with nettles woven into the fabric. Supposedly this kind of painful discipline raises ones spirits to another world while the body bleeds in this one. I do not believe it. I think it is all twaddle.

November 16, 1544
Ashridge House

... As I was saying, twaddle. Dear diary, do you know what else is twaddle? Saffron and sulfur. Kat has her face covered with a paste of saffron and sulfur. It is supposed to lighten the complexion. It stinks. This is a beauty treatment she heard of from Lady Dinsmore.

We have settled in here at Ashridge, which is the smallest of all the Houses and Palaces where I live, but this indeed is one that is a favorite for us children. Although it is only Edward and myself, as Lady Jane Grey and Robin were sent home to their families at least through Christmas. Barnaby Fitzpatrick, a great friend of

Edward's, is due to arrive in two days, as will John Cheke, our new tutor.

Edward, by the way, has been given a fool, or I should say a trial fool. His name is Florio and he is the son of one of the head Italian horse trainers. He is not that witty. It is my personal opinion that Father is trying to sneak a horseman in as a fool and thus deceive Edward into learning to ride a horse better. Edward is frightfully lacking in sporting skills and I know this pains Father.

I am now the only royal child in our family without a fool, but Father did send two minstrels, "For you, Elizabeth, for you!" He said this twice — the "for you" part. So you see I was not exiled, thank goodness. And although Ashridge is tiny by comparison, we are a jolly little household with our dull-witted fool and cozy apartments. The house indeed was once a monastery, but Father expelled all the monks five years ago. There are low ceilings and niches where relics once were placed. Again, I found in my chamber the perfect hiding place for you, dear diary. Kat's and my apartments are just off what had been the main Chapel, and there is a small slot in which the incense sticks and burners were kept. It smells so sweet and is the perfect size for a small book.

November 17, 1544

Never in my life have I heard such a shriek, and just as I was about to put pen to paper on my translation for the Queen's Christmas present — I am translating a book of French philosophical poetry for her. It is all about heaven and hell and marriage. Anyhow when I heard the shrieks I threw down my pen and I raced into Kat's chamber. "We are being poisoned! Poison! Poison!" she kept shrieking. "It's the Spaniards. I knew they always hated us. It is Princess Mary." Kat was hysterical. I took her by the shoulders, for I am nearly as tall as she, and shook her. "What are you talking about?"

"Look! Look right there!" she pointed at a plate of dainty pastries that had been sent up. I peered down at the plate and indeed saw some bright orange powder. I would have expected poison to be more subtle, at least in its physical appearance. "Don't touch it!" Kat screamed. "Oh, I don't want to die now!" she sighed. I thought it an odd remark. I suddenly spotted an overturned vial on a shelf above where the plate set. "How stupid!" I exclaimed. "How utterly stupid of you, Kat!"

Her beauty powders had overturned. Obviously, when the servitor brought in the tray, the vial tipped.

"You are not going to die, Kat, and if you keep screaming, your complexion shall turn permanently ruddy and these powders shall do you no good at all."

"Oh, Elizabeth!" she said, and raised her hand to cover her mouth in complete embarrassment.

"You are such a goose, Kat!" I walked over and embraced her.

"And you are such a good clear-brained child." We hugged. And then I had to ask her, "Kat, why did you say, 'Oh, I don't want to die now'? It is terrible to die any time when one is as young as you." She stood back from me and, still holding my shoulders, looked so sweetly into my eyes. "I am to be married to my dear friend John Ashley in the new year."

I felt a flood of such strong emotions. I was at once happy and sad. I could not hold back the thought that came first to my lips, but before it was even out Kat replied, "Fear not, Elizabeth. I shall not leave you. John will join us at Court."

And then I was truly happy and we danced around the

room and I even let Kat put the awful paste of sulfur and saffron on my face, too.

November 19, 1544

John Cheke arrived yesterday. Lessons began this morning. He is most impressed with my translations. He plans to begin Edward on some Cato, some of the shorter lyric poems. Another tutor, William Grindal, arrives shortly. I shall be working mostly with Master Grindal, and Edward with Master Cheke. This is the Queen's plan. Barnaby Fitzpatrick has also arrived. He is a terrible student and shall be working with neither tutor. Poor Kat gets stuck with him. He cannot conjugate a single Latin verb. Is that not shameful? And he is already eight! He is quite good with hawks, however, and we are planning a great hawking expedition when John Ashley comes to visit his "lady love." That is what I sometimes call Kat now. I am so excited by her betrothal. Although I know marriage is not nor ever will be for me, I think it will be good for Kat. And as long as nothing in my life is disturbed by it, I do not mind.

November 21, 1544

John Ashley, who arrived yesterday, took us all out hawk-ing after our lessons. He is a superb falconer. He teaches us how to hold our gloved arm in the proper position to launch the bird and how to give the commands.

We each take a turn in launching our birds. I love that first moment after the command is given. One can feel the change in the hawk's body. The bird seems to grow larger as its feathers plump up, and then you hear the soft rustle as it begins to spread its wings. Its heart quickens and mine, too. As if by magic the bird lifts off from your arm, and there is a part of me that always wishes to go with it. To fly!

November 23, 1544

My translation for the Queen is nearly complete. Master Grindal arrived today.

November 25, 1544

Oh, I love having a tutor all to myself. As much as I enjoyed Master Cheke, I feel that Master Grindal and I are in closer harmony in terms of the interpretation of Greek and Latin texts. I am positively racing ahead now with my New Testament translations. And this is just the first day.

November 28, 1544

After three days we — Master Grindal and I — have a fine schedule worked out for my studies. In the morning we concentrate on Greek and the New Testament translation, still accompanied by lessons in grammar. Master Grindal says that a young student might think that he has mastered grammar, but one never masters grammar. Grammar is to language as bone is to body. Without bone there is no framework for the human body and all of its marvelous organs — such is grammar to language.

November 29, 1544

I was shocked to find out that Master Grindal is not yet thirty or even close. He is but twenty-seven. He seems much older. He is completely dedicated to the purity of life. He spends much time in private meditation and does not card play or dance. I must confess that I, not knowing this, felt profound shame at first when I asked if he might make up a fourth player for a game of Gleek that Kat and John Ashley and I were intent on having. But I need not have felt this way at all, for Master Grindal is so gracious in manner. He said, "Do not worry, Elizabeth. It is my choice not to card play, but I censure no one, least of all you, in such pastimes, as I have never met a more diligent student." I was left feeling better but slightly confused. There is a part of me that thinks that perhaps I am not quite fine enough or worthy enough of such praise from such a masterful intellect.

December 5, 1544

A letter from the Queen to me today, praising my diligence, which has been reported to her by Master Grindal.

Catherine Parr really is a most excellent woman and Queen. I think of all the women my father has wed, Catherine is the most intelligent. Anne of Cleves is very smart, but I think of her more as wily than as intelligent. I think about Anne of Cleves often, and how she survived her brief marriage to my father. He did not like her at all, yet she kept her head and was given, as part of the settlement when he un-wifed her, Richmond Palace, where she now lives in lovely splendor. Now that is a smart lady. And yet she cannot hold a candle, as they say, to Catherine Parr in terms of book learning. She hardly knows Latin, no Greek, her French is abominable, her English thick as the pudding in a kid's belly. (Father once compared her accent to that.) I do hope Anne comes for Christmas to Hampton Court. She is so gay and lively. She dances a very good pavanne.

December 9, 1544

I realize, dear diary, that I have been not so faithful in my writing. Last summer I was writing daily but now it seems impossible. Master Grindal expects so much of me. There is always the New Testament translation. And then he keeps finding more and more Italian poetry for me to read. We have now begun our logic studies in earnest. So every evening I am required to prepare for the next day's lesson examples of the basic forms of logical arguments: syllogisms, tautologies, converse, inverse, and contrapositive statements. It is pleasing, however. Master Grindal allows me to make them as silly as I want. Here is my silly syllogism for tomorrow: If all men are goats, and all goats are happy, then all men are happy. I am learning the mathematical notation for expressing such arguments as well. All this needless to say keeps me extremely busy.

December 12, 1544

Weather has turned bone-cracking cold. In the schoolroom the ink freezes, and we keep two braziers filled with hot coals. Kat and John Ashley and I took hot cider today while wrapped in furs.

December 13, 1544

Still so cold. Every few minutes I must blow on my fingers or hold them to the brazier if I am to write. Master

Grindal never lets an opportunity for learning slip by. We do scientific experiments to see which freezes faster: plain water, water with salt, or wine. Plain water freezes the fastest. We still wait for the salt water and the wine.

December 15, 1544

Barnaby Fitzpatrick despite being slow in his studies is quick in other things. He begged some old venison bones from the cook and has now fashioned them into blades with his knife. With an awl he drilled small holes, through which he passed supple leather so we can fasten them to our shoes and thus we glide across the pond's ice. Edward and Henry and I must use sticks, rather like crutches for balance and support. But Barnaby whizzes round the ice as fast as anything. Edward did not stay long. He got cold and went in. He has very little spirit for sports such as these. Barnaby says that if it snows and he can beg a broad bone from the cook, like that of a cow's pelvis or shoulder, we can sled down the hills on it. There are no knight's shields here at Ashridge House. They are the best for sledding.

December 20, 1544

It begins to snow tonight. Barnaby promises he will go to the cook first thing in the morning for sledding bones. I wrap myself up in two furs and a blanket and sit by the narrow window of my chamber. It is a beautiful night. Through the falling snow we can still see the rising winter constellations. Indeed as I sit and sip the hot cider I watch through the narrow window Orion climbing in the winter sky. Orion the mighty hunter, the king, they say, of all the constellations, with more bright stars than any other heavenly grouping. If I follow the stars of his belt down and to the left, I can see Sirius, the very brightest star in the night sky, and then if I go on a diagonal upward, there is Aldebaran. Father has mapped all these stars.

December 21, 1544

The world has turned white and I am sick, bright red, Kat tells me, with fever. With fever or fury. Barnaby got his bone and all the other children go sledding. I am so angry. Why does this always happen? Kat says I am a terrible patient. She says I should not complain, as I am hardly ever sick, not nearly so often as Edward. Why can't he be sick and I well? I know that is a treasonous thought, but I really don't mean it that way. It is just that he is first of all used to being sick a great deal and handles it so well. He is an excellent patient. Second, more importantly, he does not even really care about sledding. He came in after ten minutes.

December 22, 1544

I am being a very good patient because I have no intention of missing Christmas. We leave in two days for Hampton Court. My fever is gone. Kat says I look much improved.

December 26, 1544
Hampton Court

Saint Stephen's Day. This is the best time to arrive for the Twelve Days of Christmas. The few days before everyone is so busy they have no time to pay attention to the children. But by this day the festivities are under way and people are more at their ease, no little thanks to the continuous consumption of ale. The ale barrels which are placed everywhere throughout the Palace are refilled steadily. Between the time of our arrival at the Great Gatehouse until we entered our apartments, we saw at least half a dozen troops of strolling musicians.

Once in our apartments, Kat began her usual assault, muttering the entire time such merry phrases (I jest here) as "Christmas is a deadly time at Hampton Court. . . . Too many people, too many Court leeches . . . that group Lady Dinsmore brings in here, oh, what a lot they are!" She continued muttering about all the Lords and Ladies who come to Court to impress, and how they take advantage of the King by bringing with them as many servants as possible. She is right. They bring their hounds, their horse grooms, cartloads of baggage, cages for pet ferrets, monkeys, and their hawks! It is the King who must maintain them, feed the Lords, their servitors, and even their animals.

"Riffraff!" Kat spat as she directed a servitor to go over once more a mantlepiece with a dusting cloth and told another that the pots in the closet, where we relieve ourselves, must all be taken out and scalded. She then turned to me, her face tinged pink. "To die in the stool chamber!" She squeezed her eyes shut tight with the horrific and embarrassing vision that must have seared her imagination.

She practically forbids me to breathe until every surface has been wiped clean, every oil lamp sniffed for poison powders. Kat says that poisoning through charcoal braziers and lamps is one of the most subtle ways in which a poisoner can work his evil, for the heat and rising fumes easily disperse the deadly powders. One need simply to sprinkle the poison onto the coals or stir it into the oil. "You never wake up," Kat says in a low, hard voice.

Will Somers appeared with my fiddle and a costume so I can join the musicians. My costume is that of Robin Hood — green breeches and a peaked cap! "Don't touch that fiddle!" Kat squawked and raced over with a cloth.

We are due this evening to meet with Father and Queen Catherine. I want to have time to practice a song I was learning. It was one my father had written, called "Pastime with Good Company." It has a simple melody and is the perfect song for the Twelve Days of Christmas.

December 27, 1544

Before Saint Stephen's Feast, we saw Father for the first time since we arrived. The Queen looked shimmering in a cloth of gold dress with a silver kirtle. She usually favors dark rich colors, but never anything with gilt and shine. Princess Mary has changed her hair color yet again. Too light now. And I could tell that she carried stones in her pocket in honor of Saint Stephen, who was stoned to death for blasphemy. I wonder if she will take them out of her pocket for the dancing at the revels tonight? Edward wore his new velvet suit and I my Robin Hood costume. Father was delighted. He was in very fine humor. "Come, children, come, come to this decrepit old mountain of suet and lard," he shouted, and opened his arms. One could tell he was jesting and thought himself quite handsome. So I whispered in his ear as he embraced me, "You look quite handsome, Father!" and that seemed to please him well. He stood back and pinched my cheek and winked. That wink alone was like a small gem that I tucked away. I shall remember it always. It shall glitter on the dimmest day.

He was as fat as ever quite frankly but resplendent, encrusted in gold from his doublet to his hose. Around his neck a chain of Oriental pearls hung with five great blazing rubies. Covering his nearly bald head was a flat velvet bonnet studded with emeralds, pearls, more rubies, and the snowy white plume of an egret. On his fingers he wore his customary five jeweled rings — including the star sapphire one.

We children next kneeled and kissed his hand. Kat always urges me to lick the star sapphire, as it is said to offer protection against poisoning. But I don't. I find the notion somewhat repulsive. I will not use my father and his jewels as charms against fate. If I am destined to be poisoned, I shall be, and no star sapphire shall prevent it.

Father was, of course, surrounded by members of his Privy Council and some foreign envoys. I was the last of the children to come to him. As I rose, Father smiled, then turned to a fair-haired man I had not seen before. "What thinks the Danish King of Princesses in hose and breeches?" Oh, dear, I thought, they must be thinking of a marriage for me. The Danish King, I knew, was married, so I think it was his younger brother of whom they spoke. His name was most likely Christian or Karl. It seems that all Danes are thus named if they be male.

Father noticed that I had brought the fiddle and asked

me to play. I played the song he had composed. By the end of the first verse, he joined in my singing with his thin, reedy voice. His singing voice is quite different from his speaking voice. I think his immense bulk makes it hard for him to push the air out through his own bodily pipes in rounded and melodious tones. Nonetheless he liked my singing and called me forth for another cheek pinch!

We then went into the Great Hall, where the guests had already gathered. An immense log was burning in the open fireplace. The tapestries showing the Bible story of Abraham seemed to glow in the reflected light of the fire. Thick garlands of greenery were hung in swags around the ceiling, and servitors from the kitchen stood ready in their most elegant serving costumes of Tudor green and white fringed in gold. Father, the Queen, and Edward sat on the dais. Will Somers was there, too, except that he frequently jumped up to tell a tale or a joke. I got to sit with Robin and Anne of Cleves! Robin and I had a joyous reunion, for it had been over a month since we last had seen each other. There was much good to eat. I stopped counting after nine courses that included everything from peacocks and pigeons to larks and stewed sparrows. For pastry the cooks outdid themselves with a marzipan (almond paste) replica of the Clock Court Yard complete with the astronomical clock and gilt sugar numerals!

All through the feasting, minstrels strolled, and I joined with my fiddle one small group and played, too. When the eating was finished, the tables were removed for the dancing and the masking. I noticed the Danish envoy regarding me. Your Christian or Karl shall not find a wife in me!

December 28, 1544

Father has paid for his dancing! His legs have swollen most horribly. The doctor comes to open the sores and let them drain. He lathers them in a salve of fat, ground pearl, and scorched lead, which is thought to draw out the infection.

There are no lessons during the Twelve Days. We only play.

December 31, 1544

Last day of the year and Father, as is his custom, shall receive the men and women who are suffering scrofula, the unsightly swellings and ulcers of the neck. It is believed that an anointed monarch has healing powers, so Father presses the palm of his hand on the swellings. I do not know whether it works or not.

Tonight more revels and a grand masque for which we practice with Lurcretia the Tumbler and Jane the Bald. It is the most ambitious of all maskings and was performed only once before, in the time of Mary's mother, Catherine of Aragon.

January 1, 1545

The Queen did love my gift, and it looked so lovely, for I had embroidered a cover for it with silver thread against blue cloth. She began to read it aloud upon opening it. Our masking went well although I was worried it would not. For this masque Roger Ponsby actually built England! Our emerald isle, our bright realm set in a papier-mâché sea. It was the England of Arthurian legend. Edward was King Arthur. Barnaby was Lancelot. I played Guinevere. She is the only Queen I shall ever be, with a paste crown and a scepter made from a pig's leg that was painted gold!

January 3, 1545

I am so exhausted from all the revelry and the pageants. I have thought for the first time in days about Master Grindal. He would not like any of these doings. I almost miss our orderly schoolroom. Not almost — really do. I think I shall stop writing now and just translate a few more lines of the Gospel of Saint Luke. Pray that I have not forgotten Greek entirely. Only a few more days of this intense merrymaking. It shall conclude on Twelfth Night, the rowdiest of all the celebrations.

January 7, 1545

It is over! I stayed abed until noon. No one went to Matins this morning. The Palace was as silent as a tomb. Last night, as Kat said, the revels in the Great Hall were no place a child should be. But we were, and I saw everything, I mean <u>everything</u>, and a great deal Kat is not aware of.

Everyone at the banquet wore a disguise. There were not just three Wise Men, but a half dozen, and some who dressed as camels. Kat came as the Star of Bethlehem, her dress made of cloth of silver, and she wore an immense silver star on her head. Princess Mary and I came as Nereids. Water nymphs. Father came as Neptune.

Lady Dinsmore's costume was positively scandalous. She came as a barely clad dancing girl from a sultan's harem. Lady Dinsmore's friend the Duchess of Lexford, dressed as Cleopatra, was almost as naked. I was shocked. Time and time again Robin tried while dancing to position himself so he would wind up with one of them as a partner. He finally did. I do think he made a fool of himself. I never told him that I later saw Lady Dinsmore disappear in the shadows with Robin's own father. I next saw Lady Dinsmore dancing with Henry Brandon's father. Then she disappeared with him! But that is not all. I had forgotten my fiddle, so I wandered off to find it. As I was about to enter a Privy Chamber in the Great Watching Chamber, who should exit but the Duchess of Lexford — and with, not the Duke, but Robin's father! And she was quite disheveled! There is something going on here that I almost understand, but not quite. I do have a pretty good idea, however, and I shall not mention it to Kat.

January 8, 1545

I long to get back to my studies. I am bored. I shall never teach Memo how to bowl, and what kind of goal is that, even for one who will never marry and never rule? I must cultivate my mind, but I have grown fat and lazy over these last days.

January 9, 1545

I overheard Father say something bawdy about Lady Dinsmore, and the Queen gave him a very sharp look. Master Grindal and Master Cheke arrive tomorrow so we can resume our lessons. I do not know whether we shall stay here through Candlemas Day or not. Candlemas Day is the official end to the Lord of Misrule's reign.

January 11, 1545

If men are not angels, then angels are not men — a not-so-silly syllogism. Actually not a syllogism but a contrapositive statement. A logical argument in which the second part of the statement is equivalent to the first part. Aaah!

It feels so good to be studying again. The sweet, orderly world of the schoolroom with the creamy sheets of vellum and coarser papers, the ink pot, the pale winter sun falling in shafts across my desk, the very scent of the Bible open in front of me, the curious geometry of the shapes of the Greek letters. I do love it!

January 14, 1545

We are to leave tomorrow for Enfield Palace. We have not been to this Palace for over a year. It is very small. Only seventeen rooms in all. I am so happy and relieved. I shall now confess what my worry was: that we should remain here well into February. We were at Hampton Court right after Catherine Howard was executed. She was beheaded on February 13, in 1542, and on Saint Valentine's Day we came here for a Valentine banquet. I hated it. We children were all making paper hearts and forsooth it seemed as if mine bled the blood of Catherine as I cut it. It was on the night of Saint Valentine's Day that I first heard her ghost shrieking down the Long Gallery. I just hate to be at Hampton Court for Saint Valentine's Day.

January 18, 1545
Enfield Palace

We are here, and my settling in was a great deal quicker because Kat is not here for now. She has married John Ashley. It was a small, quiet ceremony just before we left Hampton Court. She and Mr. Ashley are now off on their wedding trip for some days. Although I miss her, moving was so much simpler. Just my maid of the chamber, Mary Ward, and myself. We had everything unpacked and arranged within an hour! Kat gave extensive instructions to Mary Ward on how to check for poison.

January 26, 1545

Life is very quiet here. I enjoy my evenings in my apartments. Mary Ward is a companionable sort as she bustles about. I always thought she was so quiet but with Kat away she chats constantly. I find out all sorts of things. She told me that indeed the Lord Chancellor Thomas Wriothesley, who looks like a preserved lizard, tries to pinch her, and not on the face like Father does to me. That was why she was removed from the King and Queen's household to the children's. The Queen is mightily displeased with Wriothesley. I have always found him a most repulsive sort, even before I knew this. He has slitted eyes that bulge slightly in the manner of so many reptiles and amphibians and narrow lips that draw back into a tight grimace. One never knows whether he is about to laugh or hiss. His skin is too tight.

January 30, 1545

It is not amazing to me that Mary Ward does not read, but at first it surprised me that she had no interest in learning how. I offered to teach her letters. I am a very good teacher. I taught Edward how to read before he was three. But then Mary said to me quite simply, "Why should I read? What use would I have for it? I am a servitor and I have risen as far as one can. I assist you, Lady Princess." And then I realized how utterly logical this was. Mary Ward should not learn how to read for the same reasons I should not waste time learning statecraft. I shall never rule. I must learn to accept this. I think I am not so good at accepting things. But 'tis better to spend my energy in other, more fruitful endeavors than learning the craft of ruling. I am not quite sure what these endeavors might be, for in truth being a female third in line of succession is not an occupation. And of course a mood could at any moment descend on my father. He could exile me and make a shambles of the Act of Succession, which establishes the order of who should succeed him as ruler. It could all be over in the flickering of an eyelid. His eyelid for me.

January 31, 1545

I read some of Aesop's *Fables* aloud to Mary Ward tonight. She enjoyed them very much. I asked her again if she wanted to learn to read. She shook her head and smiled softly and then said the most astounding thing. She looked up at me and said, "I don't want to read as sure as you are that you will not marry." I was speechless. How did she know that? I asked. She said it was that night at Hampton Court. "But," I replied, "I whispered that in Robin's ear." "You did indeed, Ma'am, but then as you two little ones walked back to your apartments, I heard you muttering, when you turned a corner, 'I shall never marry.' I led you back to your chambers where Mistress

Champernowne took you in hand. You clamped your mouth shut tight and spoke no more."

"She is no longer Mistress Champernowne. She is Mrs. Ashley now."

"Yes, Ma'am, and a good soul," Mary Ward replied.

February 12, 1545

She is a good soul, but when Mrs. Ashley returned from her wedding trip the next day I could see that she was sorely troubled by the familiarity that had sprung up between Mary Ward and me. She gave me hard looks every time I used Mary's Christian name or directed anything but a command toward her. It could be a simple thing, as when on Candlemas Day I spotted a bright cardinal on a snowy branch and turned to Mary Ward and said, "What say the country folk, Mary, about a cardinal lighting on a branch outside one's window on Candlemas Day?" And Mary, forgetful of her position, instead of simply saying, "I don't know, Ma'am," replied, "Oh, Ma'am, in the country the windows of our poor cottages, if there be any, are not big enough to look out, and on Candlemas Day they would surely be closed, for we have no glass." We both laughed. Kat turned absolutely white.

My behavior in that instant was to her as shocking and scandalous as the Lady Dinsmore's. I had not exposed my bosom, but I had exposed a familiarity that was unseemly in a person of my rank. I knew it immediately. So did Mary Ward. We never spoke unguardedly again. I cannot indulge in the luxury of such familiarity. I missed it for the first few days. That is why I have not written much between my last entry and today. But now my feelings for Mary Ward fade each day a little more. I shall be fine.

Tomorrow we go to Elsynge Hall to join Father and the Queen for Saint Valentine's Day. I shall be happy. The valentines shall not bleed this year.

February 13, 1545
Elsynge Hall

The children are often the last to know. Kat warned Edward and me before we arrived here this afternoon that Father might seem distracted, as apparently the French are making trouble again. Indeed there is talk of a French invasion, and Father has spent very little time at Elsynge Palace in the past weeks but has been traveling the southwest coast with his military advisers, inspecting the coastal defenses. There is talk that the invasions will come before Midsummer's Day. Princess Mary arrived from her Palace in Beaulieu. Her hair remains the same color. I shall make a valentine for her despite our past grievances. Lucretia the Tumbler did not come with her. She has gout. But Jane the Bald came. I wonder what happens when a fool becomes too old to do tricks, to tumble.

February 14, 1545, Saint Valentine's Day
Noon

The day has not started off well at all. We were supposed to have breakfast with Father, but he was closeted with his councillors, including that old lizard Wriothesley. The King's Privy Chamber, off the social rooms of the apartment, were near enough to where we had gathered for breakfast that we could hear Father's voice booming.

"Let the Frenchies come! We'll fight them. And the Scots traitors as well! I won before. I shall again." I saw a trace of a grimace cross the Queen's face, which told me all about my father's condition. His legs must have worsened since I last saw him.

Breakfast with Father was canceled. Or rather, he took it with his Privy Councillors. We are, however, to meet him for the midday meal in another hour.

Later

I was shocked terribly when I saw Father. He was swollen to an even greater size and must have a Gentleman of the Wardrobe on either side of him as he walks with his staves. His legs are swathed in bandages that are stained. And I thought I smelled a sweet sort of foulness coming from them. The Queen ran to him immediately and lifted his legs, with the help of a gentleman of the chamber, onto a banquette. He sighed loudly and then seemed to notice us. "Oh, children! Come, come! Do not let these stinking pillars of filth repel you. Ah! Elizabeth, you have grown taller, and Edward I hope not wider." He laughed at this. Edward did not. "And Mary prettier I believe." He said this without conviction. Princess Mary would turn twenty-nine in just four days and anyone with a speck of sense knew that no woman grows prettier after twenty-five, and certainly not after thirty. It is after thirty that decrepitude begins to set in — unfortunately for women more quickly than for men.

Luncheon was attended by Sir Thomas Alsop, the royal apothecary and Father's new physician. Dr. Butts is too old now to attend him. Father, I could tell, much enjoyed his apothecary, and there was a great deal of talk about various medicines and remedies for hawks. Hawking is the only sport left that my father can really pursue now. His riding and hunting and jousting days are over.

February 15, 1545

Sometimes I wonder if we shall ever have a festive Saint Valentine's banquet again. Two years ago, it was excruciatingly grim because of the execution of Catherine Howard. Last year I had been exiled, and Kat tried to make a cheery evening of it for me at Hatfield. Now this year there is the threat of a French invasion and of course Father's health. Yet we all arrived in the banqueting house wearing a touch of red or more. Will Somers was dressed as Cupid and Jane the Bald had hearts painted on her head. The

Saint Valentine's banquet had all the appearances of a festive occasion.

There was a pageant following the banquet. "Yet another occasion for Lady Dinsmore to display herself," hissed Kat when we returned to our apartments.

February 19, 1545
Enfield Palace

We returned to Enfield today. We were required to stay at Elsynge through Princess Mary's birthday. Father gave her a lovely sapphire pendant. I could see Mary was quite touched. I have decided that the true lovers of this Valentine's season are Kat and John Ashley. They behave so sweetly and delicately with each other. Kat has no need for the wiles and false charms of Lady Dinsmore. I saw Kat and John Ashley walking together in the gardens. You would never have guessed it was the middle of winter. They looked as bright and cheerful as if they were out Maying. I can't wait for May Day. It is, I believe, my favorite holiday. Nothing else can compare. Easter to my mind is rather grim, and all the grimmer if Princess Mary is around. She goes into such contortions over Easter.

People get too emotional about religion, even my father. I love God, but I don't know if it really matters to me if other people love Him in the same way I do.

February 22, 1545

We go to Hatfield tomorrow. Robin Dudley will join us there. I am so happy. To be at Hatfield when not banished and with Robin is a dream come true, for truly Hatfield is my favorite of all dwelling places. Barnaby Fitzpatrick shall come, too. I am not sure Kat welcomes this as he is such a poor student.

February 24, 1545
Hatfield

Shrove Tuesday, the last day of Shrovetide and the day before Ash Wednesday. Very long Matins. During Matins, Barnaby Fitzpatrick made an embarrassing noise as one might hear in a barnyard, and we all started giggling. I wished Princess Mary had been here. She would have had a fit.

February 25, 1545

Ash Wednesday. Just as the priest dabbed the ashes on my forehead, someone again made a barnyard noise. I think it was Robin this time. We were all once more helpless with giggles.

Later

We are in trouble for our unseemly behavior in the chapel. We are required to kneel and say a long list of prayers and psalms for an hour. All of us! Edward and I think it is not at all fair. We did not make these noises. It is not our fault.

February 27, 1545

Found the old hiding place for you, dear diary. The loose panel in the floor of my wardrobe cabinet had been occupied by a mouse in my absence. I dusted it out and slipped you in. Hope the mouse does not return and chew you up.

February 28, 1545

One of those teasing late winter days made to fool one into thinking it is spring. The sun shines so fiercely that one is tempted to go outside without a cloak. The earth is all loose and mud sucks eagerly at one's footsteps. Robin and I rode the ponies hard after lessons and came back mud splattered. I had to take everything off and hand it to Mary Ward for either washing or brushing. Kat declares my stockings ruined.

Hatfield is quite comfortable for Kat and John Ashley. Their apartments next to mine are large and commodious and have several fireplaces. I like having Mr. Ashley in our little group. He is well-tempered and quite smart, I think. When he married Kat and became an official member of the Court, he was put in charge of the accounts for the children's households. This means keeping track of all the expenses for running our households, from the food on our table to the salaries for the tutors and the monies for our books and papers and pens and ink.

March 3, 1545

Remember how I told you John Ashley was smart and tended the household accounts? Well, I overheard him and Kat talking about Wriothesley. They suspect him of some moneymaking scheme that is improper — profiting off the King's household accounts. It is about something that is not his to sell, yet he sells it. It could be anything — food from the royal kitchens or even minor jewels. I'm not sure. I could not hear everything they said. But John Ashley suspects him. So yet another reason to detest the Lizard!

March 7, 1545

Edward is quite ill. He has a high fever and catarrh of the chest. He coughs and breathes raspily. An envoy was sent on the fastest horse to Greenwich, where Father is now in residence, to fetch the royal physicians and apothecaries and a surgeon if need be.

March 8, 1545

I am really worried about Edward. I sit beside him and read to him. He finds my company soothing, and when I am not reading, I am praying. If — can I dare say the words? But if Edward should die, I do not know what might happen to me with Princess Mary as Queen. The thought stills my blood. It is not right to pray for him for only these selfish reasons. In truth, I do love Edward. For all his bossy ways I should feel desolate if he were to leave me. I taught him how to read. I made him his first cambric fancywork shirt. I even, in secret, taught him how to stitch on an embroidery frame one day, although it is not thought manly and Father would have exiled me if he had known. But Edward begged, and in his bossy way said, "I shall be King and I thereby command you to teach me to stitch." Never was such a command issued in the realm. And then he kissed me when I taught him and promised never to tell. And he will not, for he is a boy of honor. Oh, dear God, do not take Edward! My dear little Prince.

March 9, 1545

The royal physicians arrived very late last night. Thomas Alsop, the apothecary, and Edward Rogers, who had trained with Dr. Butts and now tends to my father, are here along with a surgeon. I was summoned before Matins this morning to Edward's apartments for he had called for me. I did start, however, when I walked in the chamber and saw Archbishop Cranmer. No one had mentioned anything about the Archbishop coming. They truly must be expecting Edward to die, for why else would the Archbishop be there, I thought, but to give dear Edward last rites? I sat down next to Edward and took his hand. "I am here, Edward," I whispered. "You will get better. You must will it in your heart and your brain." His lips, all dry and cracked, tried to say something back, but he could not gather the wind for speech. Still he heard me. The physicians said this is a good sign. I sat there all morning. They bled him once. They had laid on his chest a poultice of pulverized licorice root, pennyroyal, and mustard. This is the favored method of dissolving the catarrh that causes mucus in the lining of the lungs and throat. They discussed endlessly every illness Edward has ever had, which are numerous for his seven short years. He has had: quinsy or choking tonsil illness, jaundice, green sickness, gnawings in the belly, worms, and a variety of coughs and agues. Ague is a terrible shivering and shaking of the bones accompanied by a very high fever. I have only ever had coughs and common colds.

March 10, 1545

Edward's fever has broken! He is through the crisis. Word has been sent to Father. We all go to the Chapel and make prayers of thanksgiving. When a Prince or a King is sick nothing is normal, and through these confusing days we all but forgot about little Barnaby Fitzpatrick. I finally found him on the day the physicians and apothecary came. He was crying in a corner, and you'll never believe what he said. "If Edward dies, Elizabeth, I shall never get to be whipping boy. I mean, of course, your father would have to die, first, so that Edward would be just a boy King." You see if the King is still a child and misbehaves, he, of course, cannot be whipped. So there is appointed a royal whipping boy. I blushed with shame when I thought that here Barnaby was worried about <u>not</u> getting whipped if Edward died, and here I was worrying about getting whipped or worse by Princess Mary should she succeed my father as King. Barnaby Fitzpatrick has a large heart for someone so young.

March 20, 1545

Today I get out of bed for the first time in ten days. No sooner had the doctors left than I, too, was stricken by the same catarrh as Prince Edward. They were not, however, called back for me. For the third in line to the throne, they run to the village and get the local doctor — one Geoffrey Smollet. They told Smollet exactly the course of treatment Edward Rogers and Thomas Alsop had prescribed for Edward, and then he did the same for me — including the bleeding, which I hate. I made myself watch as they opened the vein in my ankle and drew out the blood with the cup and the straw. I felt if I can watch this I shall not be frightened of anything. Not of dying, nothing. Not even Mary. The thought of Mary being Queen and not me — of my being Mary's subject — is almost more frightening than the thought of dying.

March 21, 1545

The sun is strong today. It streams through my window. I get up for the first time and make my way to the school-room where Master Grindal awaits me. During my illness he paid many visits to my chamber and read to me.

Later

It was such a strange feeling walking after these ten days in bed. My legs, my feet, felt quite unfamiliar and rather insubstantial. Each step felt so odd, as if I were floating.

March 22, 1545

Edward and I were permitted to go outside today in the garden as the weather was so warm and the sun shining. One can tell that the earth is slipping from the grip of winter. The ground feels soft underfoot. Barnaby and Robin race ahead. Edward and I are still too weak to run.

March 24, 1545

This is the first day I really feel my old self. I want to go hawking tomorrow with John Ashley and Robin and Barnaby. Kat says, "We'll see." "We'll see" often means no.

March 25, 1545

I'm right. It was no and I am furious. We have had one beautiful day after the next. It seems as if spring is in a rush to get here, and Edward and I sit inside all day long. For the first time ever I am bored with my studies. I am now well into translating the Gospel of Saint Matthew from Greek, but I care not for the endeavor. I have suggested to Master Grindal that we commence some natural history studies. Perhaps we could go outside collecting. "Collecting what?" he asks. I am not sure. So I say the first thing that pops into my mind: "Butterflies." He reminds me that it is much too early for butterflies. I think again. "Earthworms. There must be many earthworms beginning to stir," I say. He says he will think upon it. That is like Kat saying, "We'll see."

March 26, 1545

Released at last. It has been decided that we can go out-doors for what Master Grindal and John Cheke call natu-ralizing. We go armed with bottles and collecting nets, and jugs, and a few pasteboard boxes. I am to collect earth-worms since they were my idea. Robin and Barnaby are collecting insects. Edward shall look for buds and grow-ing things. There seems to be more variety in what the boys are collecting. As far as I can see all earthworms are the same. They perhaps vary in length and circumference. That is all. They are all a fleshy pink. When I say this, Master Grindal says, "Ah, but, Princess, you must culti-vate a naturalist's eye. You must learn to observe." Then he picks up worms I have collected and immediately points out at least five or six differences. "And their behavior you must observe, too." This bewilders me. I have never thought of worms having behavior. Master Grindal is going to show me how to do experiments. That sounds exciting.

March 27, 1545

Barnaby, although slow with his schoolroom work, proves himself a born naturalist. He has found an amazing variety of beetles. He makes wonderful drawings of them. One can cut an earthworm in half and it still wiggles. My experiment is to cut two earthworms in half. With one earthworm, I put the two halves in separate but identical environments. With the other, I put the two halves in contrasting environments. I am then to observe how they behave. This is a very different kind of learning from what we have ever done before.

March 28, 1545

There is still much talk about the invasion of the French. I hear Kat and Mr. Ashley talking about it all the time, and often Masters Cheke and Grindal. Today Master Grindal and Master Cheke taught us all together, and we studied a map of the southeast coast. *Great Harry,* the flagship, and the other immense ship, the *Mary Rose,* are now at Portsmouth along with the rest of the English fleet. Master Grindal explained to us how there is a system of beacons along the coast in all of the villages that the citizens light to warn of invasion. We all wish we could go to the coast and help with the beacons. It sounds so exciting.

March 29, 1545

Soon we depart for Windsor Castle. We shall spend Holy Week there. None of us likes Windsor much. It is so boring. No galleries, no gardens. The rooms are bare compared to our other Palaces and Houses. And the bedchambers and our apartments are too large to be cozy. I hope we do not have to stay there long.

April 5, 1545
Windsor Castle

We arrived last night. Today is Palm Sunday. All of Court is here.

April 9, 1545

Maundy Thursday we eat hot cross buns. I take a great time picking the sugar cross off the bun and eating it as slowly as possible. Edward when no one is looking licks his cross off. It is interesting no one notices what I do, or perhaps they do not care, but picking off the sugar cross is just as ill-mannered as licking it off. I am rarely corrected when I am with Edward, and it is not because I am a better or more polite child. I am just invisible, as I have already explained. Sometimes it seems as if I am more invisible than others. That is why I love it when Father winks at me or pinches my cheek. I am a horder of my father's winks, a miser with his pinches. I would trade every single one of my royal jewels, and I do have a few, for a chest full of winks!

After mass this morning, we follow Father to where he will wash the feet of beggars as our Lord Christ did at the Last Supper. It is the custom of Kings to wash as many beggars as the King is old. So my father must wash fifty-three pairs of feet. He cannot lower himself to his knees this year, so they bring a chair and he lifts the feet onto his lap. This is my favorite part of Holy Week. I love to see how the beggars watch their King with such wonder and absolutely no fear and I love to look at the beggars' feet. They could almost not be feet they are so different from mine. Many are blackened and calloused, some cracked. I see gnarled toenails and some with no toenails. Some run with pus and others bleed. But for each beggar my father takes great care. He pours on the water to first rinse the caked dirt and then from another bowl he takes soapy water mixed with lavender and gently scrubs the feet. A final rinse with the oil-scented water and then a fresh cloth to dry them.

April 10, 1545

Good Friday. We fast all day and then go to Chapel, where we read the Passion of our Lord Jesus and all about his suffering on the cross. Every time Pontius Pilate's name is read in the service, Princess Mary makes this painful little grimace. She has changed her hair again. It is a dusty red color now. Most unbecoming.

April 12, 1545, Easter Sunday

I often wonder how Edward feels when we are in the Chapel here at Windsor. For this is where his mother, Jane Seymour, is buried. Right in the floor of Saint George's Chapel. I think I am glad my mother is buried far away. I mean, can Edward think about God in this Chapel? We come to celebrate the Resurrection, but I cannot help but think of the most loathsome aspects of death and of the funerary sciences. Robin has told me much, for when his grandmother died he learned all about it. When a person of high rank dies, it is the practice to do everything to preserve the body as long as possible. First, they make a brew of spices and soak the body for several days. Next, they wrap the dead person tightly in bandages of special cloth that have been tarred and covered with molten lead. Finally, they put the body into a box and that box into another, the coffin. I think of Edward's mother all wrapped up and spiced and, well, it is very hard to pay attention to the Archbishop.

April 19, 1545

I simply cannot understand why we have to be here so long. It has something to do with the French. For Father perhaps it is not so bad, for he has several hunting lodges around here, and although he no longer hunts he goes there to escape the Court at times. We are never invited! We have to stay here in this stinking old bleak castle. I hate it. And I hate going to Chapel. All I think of is poor Queen Jane all spiced up and wrapped in lead. I think my humors are out of balance. But I am afraid to tell anybody because they always come and bleed you!

April 20, 1545

Hooray! We may leave. We now go to Greenwich for Saint George's Day. This is my father's royal birthday, for he was crowned on that day, April 23, thirty-six years ago.

And then soon it shall be May Day. Oh, dear God, I hope the French don't invade before May Day and ruin it.

April 25, 1545
Greenwich Palace

I do notice one thing. Since Kat has married John Ashley, she does not go into such fits over poisoners. Our settling in is accomplished without all the frenzy and hubbub, as the Scots say. I do love that expression, "hubbub." One of the better things we got from the Scots. Although Edward says he thinks golf, also from the Scots, sounds most amusing. I am doubtful of sports that attract Edward,

though. He lacks the temper for a pastime requiring true
vigor.

April 27, 1545

Lady Dinsmore has had the smallpox! She contracted it
shortly after Valentine's Day. A pocked Venus! She is ruined. Absolutely ruined. What else did Lady Dinsmore
have aside from her beauty? I doubt if she is a great lyric
poet. It is not a question really of what she will do, for
what do any of us females do? It is really a question of
what will give her satisfaction. Nothing, I think. There is
very little satisfaction to be gotten for a scarred beauty in
the Court of my father.

Lady Jane Grey arrived today, just in time for the May
Day celebrations. She has grown so much taller. She is still
rather short, however.

April 28, 1545

We children are hatching a plan. We want to be able to go
into the countryside before daybreak on the first of May,
just as the village children do, and into the woodlands to

gather leafy branches and make nosegays and crowns of flowers. It would be so much fun. We are composing a letter to Father for permission. Kat says he is so distracted now with the French, he might not have time to read it.

April 29, 1545

Word came back through Father's councillor Sir Anthony Denny. Everyone might go Maying at the dawn except for Prince Edward. Edward threw a fit! I honestly think he was prepared to give up his crown for this. The foggy vapors at dawn are considered too dangerous for his fragile health. I am caught between a terrible conflict of emotions: being terribly sad for Edward but overjoyed at my own good fortune.

Robin says I am being a goose. He says Edward would never enjoy it as much as the rest of us anyhow. So I should stop worrying and think of my own pleasure. I shall bring Edward something special back from the expedition.

April 30, 1545

I am so excited tonight that I shall never be able to sleep. Mary Ward has been given instructions to wake me at three hours after midnight. I have never in my entire life risen so early. She has laid out my clothes. I am to wear a heavier cloak than usual, as it will be cold at that early hour. I must try to go to sleep now. I wonder if Robin and Lady Jane Grey and Barnaby are having trouble sleeping?

May 1, 1545

It was pitch-black when I rose. Mary Ward had brought me a steaming mug of cider. John Ashley and I met the others at the south gate and then, to our utter surprise, who appears but Jane the Bald, her head painted once more with flowers. She quickly put on a bonnet, however, for a terrible chill hung in the air. We proceeded through the gate. We had not walked two hundred yards from the palace when we encountered our first group of village folk. The darkness began to lighten. And then the first streaks of the sun's light spilled low over the horizon tingeing the earth a soft pink. It was beautiful watching the mists of night disappear and the morning fill with color. Every blade of grass stood out sharply.

A village girl fell into line beside me. Her name was Mandy and she was about my age and had been Maying ever since she could remember. I know she took me for just a normal girl; perhaps well-born but certainly not a Princess, which was perfect. She showed me where great rafts of myrtle grew, which she said was the best for making flower crowns.

By ten the sun was full up and it was very warm. We turned to go back to the village. As we passed one gate, Mandy went through. "Where are you going?" I asked. "Home," she laughed. "You live here?" It was a mean little cottage. A pig routed in a muddy yard, and some very young kittens tumbled in the one patch of grass.

I pushed back my cap for it was frightfully hot now and I saw her face freeze. Indeed it was as if she were looking at something terrible. A witch perhaps. "What's wrong?" I asked. Her mouth moved, but no words came out. And then a breeze blew a strand of my red hair across my face, and I knew what it was. She had recognized me. Everyone knows I have red hair like my father. So even if my likeness has not been painted as often as Edward's, Mandy somehow knew. She curtsied deeply. "You are the Princess Elizabeth, My Lady." But I knew from the way she had looked in my face that her first thought had been that I was the daughter of the witch Anne Boleyn. The country-folk in particular hated my mother. I nodded.

Then I noticed a man come into the yard. He was scooping up the kittens and putting them in the gunny-sack. "What does he with those kittens?" I asked. "He takes them to be drowned, My Lady." She curtsied again. "Drowns them?" I was bewildered. "Why?" "Too many." The man overheard and came up and tousled Mandy's hair affectionately. "You can drown the kitties, but not the kids," he laughed. "Might I have one, sir, to take to my brother?" Suddenly the same shocked look streaked through his eyes. "Yes . . . yes . . . My Lady," he stammered and reached in the sack and drew out a little mar-malade-colored kitten. "Thank you," I said.

Edward was most pleased with the kitten. He names it Aesop. Must stop writing for the May games and tournaments begin soon.

May 2, 1545

After the games, we went to the newly constructed "banquet house" all made from leafy boughs, and it was here that we took our meal. When we finished, we heard toots on horns then giddy laughter. Before our eyes a maypole rose and a score of ruddy village girls stormed in and began dancing around the pole. Mandy was one of them. I wanted to call out and wave, but I knew I could not. I wanted so badly to tell somebody, anybody, that I knew one of the May dancers, that I had been Maying with that one there, with the flaxen hair. Will Somers danced in and out of the May girls and carried a long silver ribbon that he twined around their waists until by the end they indeed were all laced together. I wanted to be part of that; to be laced with silver ribbon to these village girls. If I can't be Queen I think, quite honestly, I would rather be a village maid with a yard tumbling with cats. Is that not a queer thought?

I had many queer thoughts as I watched the dancers. I think it is indeed the condition of a Princess to always be set apart from such things, to feel separate and alone. I thought of Mary Ward and the few words and thoughts we had shared during the brief time when Kat was away. I thought, too, of Lady Dinsmore, now shuttered in some dark chamber of the Palace, running her long fingers over the pits and bumps of her once flawless skin. They say she never comes out in daylight, and in the evening she always wears the heaviest of veils. She allows no lamps or torches burning near her, but only the slenderest of tapers. How can she even read?

May 8, 1545

The talk and the tension increases daily concerning the French invasion. We children are to be moved shortly, and Father and the Queen will go to Portsmouth.

May 10, 1545

Father has sent more men to the south coast. There are now nearly one hundred thousand armed men there and over one hundred ships of the royal fleet at anchor near The Solent off Portsmouth.

Meanwhile our astronomical studies continue on the

roof of the palace, as these spring nights are clear and we can spy Jupiter rising and Mars burning hot and red. The giant and the warrior command the heavens, and my father here on earth makes ready for war.

September 1, 1545

Dear diary, at last we are reunited! I cannot believe what a fool I am. We had to leave Greenwich of a sudden. Father decided that, with the threat of the French invasion, he wanted us children tucked away in the country. So we were sent to Hatfield. In the flurry of the packing up, I completely forgot you tucked beneath the loose stone under my bed! I could not fetch you myself and I could hardly send someone to look for you. So I had to wait nearly four long months until we cycled back to Greenwich. I am pleased to say I found you exactly where I left you and seemingly undisturbed.

It has been now over a year since I began writing on your pages. Within that year, I have been returned to Court from exile, then exiled again, then brought back once more. I am a year older. Some things come easier —

Greek, Latin. Some things are just as hard — loneliness and the nearly constant want, or is it need, for my father's attention — his cheek pinches and kisses.

I suppose what I did spare you by leaving you at Greenwich was a lot of complaining. You see Hatfield is simply too small for both Princess Mary's household and mine together. I had to give up my friends. Barnaby, Robin, Lady Jane all sent away. Princess Mary, of course, got to keep Jane the Bald and Lucretia the Tumbler. They certainly earned their keep, as Mary was in a most foul mood all summer. Any wedding plans with Charles V's, the Holy Roman Emperor's, nephew Dom Luis are off.

September 2, 1545

How self-centered I am! My entry yesterday was filled with complaints and petty grievances about Princess Mary. I daresay I neglected the most important event of the summer: The French and the sinking of the *Mary Rose*! Next to *Great Harry*, the *Mary Rose* is the grandest ship in the English fleet. My father and the Queen went to Portsmouth in July. Shortly after their arrival, the French fleet was spied and the warning beacons were lit. From a promontory Father watched what was expected to be a minor naval engagement as the *Mary Rose* sailed out to meet the French. She had just fired all her cannons on her starboard side, making her light on that side, when a freak gust of wind caught her sails aback. She rolled over immediately and sank!

"It was but a moment!" That is what Father keeps saying about the *Mary Rose*. And then there was the second great tragedy. Just on the heels of the sinking of the *Mary Rose* came the news that my father's lifelong and closest companion, Charles Brandon, the Duke of Suffolk, had died of heart seizure.

My father is not well. He is in deepest melancholy. And this is strange — I now love him most. He is enormously fat. He growls constantly. His legs stink, but he has lost his best friend and he is like a lost boy himself. How can I help but love him? He is no longer simply King, or Father, or the husband of six wives. He is friendless. And so I should be if Edward or Robin or now even Barnaby were taken from me.

September 6, 1545

Tomorrow is my birthday. I turn twelve. I know not if
there shall be a celebration or gifts of any sort, as everyone
is most concerned with Father. But this does not disturb
me. For I know how lucky I am. You realize, dear diary,
Princesses have been married off at twelve. Not me thank
heavens. So I think I shall celebrate tomorrow the fact
that I am not betrothed or married. That is gift enough.
Odd that Mary would celebrate if she were betrothed. But
there lies the difference between us.

September 7, 1545

My birthday was not entirely forgotten. The Queen gave
me a lovely bound copy of the writings of Aristotle, which
I begin to study now with my tutor. Father gave me a gift
from the Jewel House. It is a bracelet enameled with his
motto, *Dieu et mon droit,* or God and my right. It is much
too large for my wrists. I do not mean to sound ungrateful
but you know me well enough, dear diary, that I can say to
you that I would have much preferred a wink or a pinch

from my father to this bracelet, which simply jiggles around on my rather thin wrist.

September 16, 1545

A surprising turn of household events. Father apparently is feeling much better and goes to his hunting lodge at Woodstock, and we children are to accompany him! I wonder how many Gentlemen of the Privy Council will go with him. Many do not like Woodstock, as it is old and the river marshes often smell. But I do not mind it.

September 25, 1545
Woodstock

It is always a guessing game here as to which rooms we shall occupy. Many are uninhabitable due to water damage from leaking roofs or crumbling plaster. It was here at Woodstock that I first held a crossbow and shot it. Father is so much better, and he promises that every day shall be devoted to what he calls the two h's — hunting and hawking. Our tutors are not even here. We must, says the

Queen, study on our own for now and learn the most challenging discipline of all — to become our own masters in regard to our studies. Prince Edward and I are required to submit a plan of independent study each morning for our time here at Woodstock.

Here is mine for the first day:

Morning Lessons

8:00–8:30: Review Aristotle's system of animal classification.

8:30–9:00: Devise four statements of logic that reflect the truths of the classification system.

9:00–9:30: Read and translate at least two pages of Cicero.

9:30–10:00: Read Epistles of Saint Paul.

10:00: HAWKING WITH FATHER!

Afternoon Lessons

3:00–4:00: Read Virgil and try to compose some lines in the Virgilian meter — dactylic hexameter.

4:00–4:30: Read Scripture.

I think it is a good plan.

September 27, 1545

He winked! He winked! Father winked at me! Mary had dyed her hair again and I made some comment. As soon as it was out I was regretting it, for I thought Father would be angry, but no, quite the opposite. He winked at me and then said something about how a dye would never subdue my ruddy hair. And then, you shall never believe it, he reached across the table and pinched my cheek, and I can still feel the pinch. Oh, I am in heaven!

September 28, 1545

Ours days here fall into an easy rhythm. I like it well this place despite the dampness and the crumbling plaster. Kat complains endlessly, but I do believe Woodstock is much to the liking of John Ashley. We hawk or hunt each day and the Lizard is not here! Tomorrow is Michaelmas Day. A banquet is planned. Last year's celebration when we celebrated the fall of Boulogne seems so far away.

October 1, 1545

Today we went hunting with Father, and the Queen brought down a deer with a crossbow. Father says there is not a woman in the realm who can match the Queen with a crossbow, and many men who would be pleased to do as well. The crossbow is so hard. It is much heavier than the regular bow and arrow. It is so stiff that it must be bent by using both hands or the special winding screw. I am tall enough, apparently, but I need more weight and more muscle. Sometimes Father helps me shoot. He puts his hand over mine and helps me draw the bow. He stands behind me. When he does this, I hear an odd rasping sound in his chest. I don't think he is breathing properly. It sounds as if within this huge man there is a tiny violent one rattling at the bones. However, he can still shoot a crossbow, and he brought down four stags and three deer and a wild boar in the past week!

October 3, 1545

Oh, dear, good things never last. Father's legs swelled up horribly and began to fester.

The surgeon was called in, and Father insisted that everyone must stay. The Queen protested and said it was not a fit sight for children to see what the surgeon must do. But Father said, "No, Edward must learn to have a strong stomach. He shall see worse sights on the jousting field." There was no mention made of me. I was once again invisible. But if Edward stayed, I wanted to as well. So I watched from the shadows. The surgeon took a red-hot lancet and prodded the wound. From Father's legs came near a cup of poisonous fluids. The apothecary, Sir Thomas Alsop, stood by with folded strips of gauze that were soaked in cleansing spices, which he applied. It was an awful sight. I felt my stomach turn. I wanted to close my eyes. I wanted to bury my face in my hands, but suppose Father should look my way and suddenly I was no longer invisible? He must not see me feeling faint and squeamish as both Mary and Edward appeared to be. I must look strong. I vowed to look like the Queen I would never be. My father never cried out. He crushed the Queen's hand in his own, and I noticed only afterward that she had removed his rings. They would have cut right through the flesh to the bones of poor Catherine's thin hands.

We return to London and Whitehall tomorrow.

October 8, 1545
Whitehall Palace

The roses are fine but that is about all. Father does not do well. But Princess Mary seems to thrive, and it is for this I worry. She and Lord Chancellor Thomas Wriothesley, the Lizard, have become quite close! I like it not. I have a strange uneasiness.

October 10, 1545

My uneasiness grows. Edward and Robin and I were working in the rose garden today. Robin and I were at the far end, at a distance from Edward. I saw Princess Mary and the Lizard approach Edward. My blood froze as I saw the Lizard bend over and stroke Edward's head — Princess Mary smiling the while. One does not do this to the Prince of Wales. It is overly familiar. I saw Edward shrink back but Mary just laughed. She knows this is wrong. I think the two of them full of knavery. I immediately told Robin to go over to tell Edward we needed him. The Lizard scowled at Robin and said something rude, I could tell, but Edward seemed relieved to follow Robin. A pox on that Lizard!

October 11, 1545

Robin presses me about the Lizard and my actions yesterday. He loathes him, too, now for the Lizard actually cuffed Robin and told him he was a rude busybody just like his father! I asked Edward what the Lizard wanted, and he said nothing as far as he could tell. He just stops him all the time to chat. But Edward confessed to me that he, too, is frightened of him. Neither Edward nor I know specifically why we feel this unease, and that is why it is difficult to explain it to anybody. Even Robin. But there is no one in this Court who has my interests and Edward's more dear to his heart than Robin.

October 15, 1545

I accepted an invitation to play cards at Princess Mary's. Lucretia the Tumbler was feeling ill, and they needed a fourth. They are playing four-handed *quienela*. It is a

Spanish game. Princess Mary learned it as she did all the Spanish card games from her mother and the Spanish ambassador Chapuys. But it was not Chapuys at the card table. It was the Lizard! That is why I came, really. They told me he would be playing. And I am determined to find out what this new friendship between him and Mary is. There have been plots in the past. The Court has been swirling with these stories for years. You see, Spain has always resented how my father cast aside Princess Mary's mother who was Spanish for mine. If the Spanish were to invade and Philip, son of the King of Spain, were to marry Princess Mary, what a realm they would command. And where would the Lizard be in that grand scheme? He would love it. Lord Chancellor to the most powerful rulers on earth!

I shall share my thoughts now with Robin and see what he thinks.

October 17, 1545

Robin thinks my reasoning sound, but he says any plotters against England would first have to make sure the

Seymours were vanquished. "Vanquished?" I asked. "You mean dead?" "More or less," he replied.

One cannot be more or less dead I tell him. This I know from my most basic studies in logic. One either is dead or is not. So now we must stay alert to the health and well-being of the brothers Edward and Thomas Seymour. You, see, they were Jane Seymour's brothers, Prince Edward's uncles, and shall be really ruling for him as Regents if Father were to die and Edward were to become King while still a boy.

October 22, 1545

There is a new twist in all of this. When the King of Scots died, he left as his heir a six-day-old baby girl. She is now about three, I believe, Mary, Queen of Scots. A baby Queen! Lord Arran is her Regent. At one point two years ago or so, Edward was betrothed to Mary. But then it was broken off. Scotland is an ally of France. Lord Arran's position has grown shaky. He seeks to buttress his position of power. He seeks a marriage with Princess Mary! So, as Robin says, who cares if the betrothal between Prince

Edward and little Mary, Queen of Scots, was broken off? Another Mary might sit on that throne! They make my head swirl, these marriage plots. I asked what would happen to the baby Queen, Mary. And Robin answered quite coolly, "They would get rid of her." "You mean kill her?" I ask, then say, "Don't say 'more or less,' Robin." And he says he means kill her, or perhaps they would send her to France. But that would be a bad move, for then the French would move against Scotland to claim the throne.

Robin has learned all this simply by listening. The good thing about being a child in Court, especially a non-royal one, is that if you are clever and quiet you can learn much, for no one takes note of you. Robin is both.

October 25, 1545

Lady Jane Grey is back with us here at Whitehall. We spend pleasant sunny hours in the garden tending the roses.

October 26, 1545

A sighting! Our first of Lady Dinsmore.

Lady Jane Grey and I were in the garden at twilight.

Suddenly on the other side of a hedge we heard the crunching of gravel. Jane clutched my arm and mouthed the words "Lady Dinsmore." We both immediately crouched behind a huge stone vase. There was a gap in the hedge perfect for viewing as the heavily veiled figure of Lady Dinsmore passed by. She seemed to float, oddly detached from the world. Lady Dinsmore has no admirers now, we hear. She stays all day with her nursemaid from childhood. She serves the Queen mainly as a card partner, and we hear she is not clever at cards at all. But the Queen is too kind to turn out a Lady from Court. The Queen attempts to read to her from her own book of meditations, which she has been writing for some time now. I can only guess that she hopes to set Lady Dinsmore's mind to contemplate higher things. I think the Queen wages a losing battle. For Lady Dinsmore's entire life, her beauty was so renowned she needed only to think about her luminous skin, her comely body, her thick and shiny hair. It is hard to go inward in one's thoughts after so long a course of study of the body's surface.

November 3, 1545

Whitehall begins to stink. There is talk of Greenwich for Christmas. Kat has been going to visit Lady Dinsmore. I beg her to take me along but she absolutely won't hear of it. She accuses me of wanting to visit out of idle curiosity. I have never found curiosity idle, I tell her. She tells me I am pert with her. But why do <u>you</u> go? I ask. For she never cared much for the woman. But now she answers me, "She weepeth sore in the night, and her tears are on her cheeks: among all her lovers she hath none to comfort her (Lamentations 1:2)." Nothing infuriates me more than when people quote Scripture back to me. It stops argument, I think. How can one argue back when one's opponent has run to the Bible? Would one gainsay God? Kat thought this would shut me up. But it did not. "Well," I asked, "now that her chief rival is swathed in veils, how fares the Duchess of Lexford?" Kat's face turned dark, and for once I could not tell whether it was with fear or anger. She simply rushed out of the room, muttering about what a willful child I had become.

November 7, 1545

Father calls us children to hear some new musicians he is considering for Christmas. I realize I have been neglecting my music of late and request that Father might see fit to allow one of his musicians to instruct me further, not only on the virginal but in the making of compositions. When I ask for this, Princess Mary says she thinks it is a good idea as by the time she was my age she had composed several pieces. The Lizard was there, and when Princess Mary said this, they both smiled loathsome little private smiles. I say again, these two are full of knavery.

November 9, 1545

The weather has suddenly turned freezing cold. Immense logs now burn in the hearths, and the heat stirs anew the foul smells. I hope we leave soon. When Lady Jane Grey and I took a turn in the garden, we noticed that the roses were glazed in thinnest skins of ice. Jane wanted us to cut them and bring them in and save them, but I thought there was a startling beauty to these ice-sheathed roses. I knew that they would turn black within hours and die, but for now they were radiant, for indeed they reflected the pale November sun. I am much interested in laws of reflection and refraction, as a matter of fact. We study this with Master Grindal. But for now I shall enjoy how this weak November light shimmers on the rose's icy petals. There is an unnameable glory in such things, though they live only for a moment and turn black within the hour.

November 10, 1546

Master Grindal took us to the roof of Whitehall Palace tonight to observe the night heavens. It was clear, moonless, and so cold. But Cassiopeia is now near the celestial meridian, and Pegasus begins its rise into the wintry sky. A thin sheet of ice lays on the Thames, catching the reflection of the stars.

November 11, 1545

Saint Martin's Day again. Princess Mary as usual slogging about in her shredded cloak. We all have our noses buried in pomander balls.

November 13, 1545

Father did pay attention to my request, and I now study several hours a week with William Allen, one of Father's favorite Court musicians. He gives me small, very specific exercises in composition. He urges me to grow bold with the melodies. I try. I protested that I am not a bold person, and he looked me straight in the eye and said, "That is sheer twaddle, My Lady." This makes me think. I wonder if I am bold? But how can an invisible Princess be bold? If I were so bold, I would not be forgotten as often I am. But there is something within me that makes me think that perhaps I could be bold. It almost feels like a seed deep in my heart, or is it my brain? Perhaps boldness is both a part of the heart and the brain. I do feel that if this seed were planted in the right soil, it might possibly grow.

November 18, 1545
Westminster Palace

We are here but briefly at Westminster Palace. Just a few weeks before we go to Greenwich for Christmas. We came here to breathe! The air was so foul at Whitehall. I have to find a hiding place for you, diary, for I have not visited this palace since you came into my hands. There is in this chamber, once occupied by a Lady-in-Waiting of Catherine of Aragon, a small wall niche in which was placed a reliquary, a box for a relic — a scrap of a saint's bone or lock of hair. The box is still there but empty, and perfect in size. I shall put you inside.

November 19, 1545

I came back from my lessons today to hear voices being raised in the receiving rooms of my apartments. When I entered, I saw Princess Mary holding my reliquary! My heart nearly leaped from my chest, for I knew that in it was my diary. Princess Mary claimed that the reliquary belonged to her mother and that it was hers by right of inheritance. Kat was saying that she could never let anything be removed without my permission.

I was absolutely white with fury. But I knew that quick revenge was but a fleeting reward. I must maneuver Mary into a position of vulnerability and fear. I quietly said, "And, Princess Mary, did you find a saint's bones in the reliquary?" She mumbled and blushed bright red to the roots of her yellow hair. She held out the reliquary toward me. "Here. Take it." This was going to be her way out, or so she thought. John Ashley and Mary Ward had come into the room, having heard the commotion. Princess Mary moved for the door to leave. "<u>Stop</u>!" My voice sliced the air like a finely tempered sword. "There is only one person who could have put you up to this, Princess Mary." Now I saw the color drain from her face. "You are thick with him, are you not? You play cards with him. Not only that, you have taught him how to cheat. Oh, you are full of knavery the two of you."

One could have heard a pin drop. "And how go your plans for marriage to Lord Arran? And what will you do with the baby Queen, Mary of Scots? There is talk of a renewal of the betrothal between Mary, Queen of Scots, and our brother, Edward." I just made this up. But it scared Mary, I could tell. She <u>had</u> contemplated the murder of the baby Queen just as Robin had said. But a baby Queen married to Edward would require two murders!

"You are speaking treason." I had never mentioned the death of a Queen or a Prince, but she had thought of it. This is treason. It was written all over her face. And everyone knew it.

"If you go to Father, he will not believe a word you say," she replied.

"Do not worry, Mary. I shall not tell Father anything — oh, perhaps, if you and that loathsome little Lizard of a Lord Chancellor <u>ever</u> invade my privacy again, I shall tell Father just one thing."

"What be that?"

"I shall tell him that you and the Lord Chancellor together cheat at cards. That is all."

Princess Mary gave a small yelp and clutched her hands. With good cause she made these gestures. My father hates beyond anything a cheat. The last man caught cheating in a game with the King had the fingers of his right hand chopped off. And my father took his rings in payment for the money he had lost at cards.

November 20, 1545

I was, needless to say, left agitated from my encounter with Mary. I could not sleep. What kept me up most were torturous thoughts about my diary. Did she read any of it? How did she know it was there? She and the Lizard were looking for something. And now I have another problem. She knows about you, dear diary, so where might I hide you? For two nights, I have slept with or carried you along with me in a small drawstring purse, but this cannot go on. It is simply impractical.

November 21, 1545

I think I have solved the problem of a hiding place. I have thought of the last place Princess Mary and the Lizard would look if they ever dare to break in here again. It is the reliquary. They would of course expect me to find a new place. So the safest place is the old place. The reliquary has a simple metal clasp. I shall thread a strand of my hair through the eyes of the clasp and in this way I can tell if it has ever been disturbed.

November 26, 1545

Anthony Scorsby is the new Lord of Misrule for the holidays, and we are all so pleased, for he brought us children together for what he called a consultation of merriment and what the children in particular would like for the Twelve Days of Christmas. We all of course, except for Lady Jane, said Chase the Pig. Sir Anthony said, "Of course. But that is not original. Think harder, children." So we shall.

November 27, 1545

We go to Greenwich soon but the river is frozen, so we shall have to go by land. It takes much longer.

Have I mentioned that Princess Mary has been avoiding me completely?

November 28, 1545

Lucretia and Jane the Bald both came to me today and begged me to come and play cards. They say that they hate the Lord Chancellor and he is there all the time; that he misbehaves toward Mary's chambermaids and they are at their wits' end. I tell them I cannot go. I do not say why. I want them to have no information that would make them vulnerable to the Lizard. This is a difficult situation. I feel for Jane and Lucretia.

December 15, 1545
Greenwich Palace

What is it? Every Christmas I am sick. I have had the most violent stomach pains and retching.

December 16, 1545

Nothing to write. All is boring.

December 19, 1545

My first well day and where am I allowed to go? To Princess Mary's apartments to play cards! Princess Mary complimented me about something. I am worried. Maybe I still look sick. Maybe she thinks I am going to die. A worse thought: Maybe Father has pinched her cheek or winked at her during my illness. She has seen much more of him than I have recently. I cannot bear the thought of Father giving winks to Mary. I would give up everything if I knew he would never wink at her. I am the only one who really deserves the winks. I am the only one who truly understands his humor, his music. This is not fair. I must be calm.

December 24, 1545

It is two hours before midnight, and I ready myself for the solemn mass that shall officially begin the Twelve Days of Christmas. We go to the Chapel Royal. I have especially asked that Master Grindal be invited, but now I am somewhat worried as it is a very splendid and glittering service. Master Grindal I think will disapprove. Father is the head of the Church of England. That is not being Catholic, and it is not quite Protestant, but Master Grindal has definite reformist ideas. The reformers like to pray simply. It is a great honor, however, to be invited to the midnight mass, and I could think of no other way to honor my esteemed tutor. I hope he understands.

Later

The Chapel was lit with one thousand tapers, and the gold stars in the blue ceiling glittered in their reflected light. I think Master Grindal was actually most pleased that he had been invited. Princess Mary weeps excessively at these services, and I caught Master Grindal looking at her oddly. I gave him a quick little smile and a wink. I wanted to reassure him that I feel such displays are worse than twaddle.

December 26, 1545

It is late and I am exhausted from the Saint Stephen's Day feast, but we had a most surprising visitor: The Earl of Arran! And he was seated next to Princess Mary!

Still Later

I had to crawl back under my bed and get you, dear diary, from your hiding place beneath the loose floor stone. An amazing revelation tonight. Mary Ward came in to bank my fire. We have not spoken familiarly for almost a year now, but I could not help but notice a curious little smile on her face. So I had to ask her what was so funny. It took a little coaxing, but she finally told me. It seems she accidentally interrupted a romantic tryst! She happened upon the Duchess of Lexford and Lord Arran in a passionate embrace in a small alcove near the Chapel!

December 27, 1545

Although there are many fewer people here at Greenwich than at Hampton Court, as it is smaller, the merrymaking is just as vigorous and seems to mount each day. My best memory of the Christmas will be the musicians. I joined one group with my fiddle, and William Allen plays, too. We wander all the halls and corridors. I do notice how in the daylight Lord Arran stays as far away from the Duchess of Lexford as possible, and I might add is quite attentive to Princess Mary.

January 6, 1546

The Duchess of Lexford is dead. She has been poisoned! I shall write more later.

They found her in the Chapel the morning after the Twelfth Night banquet.

January 7, 1546

Kat has collapsed in a state of apoplexy. She screams that when I was sick she is sure it was poison. But I am alive. She gets so hysterical that John Ashley has called the apothecary to dose her with tincture of poppies.

January 9, 1546

All is in disarray since the poisoning. Father is sending me to Hatfield, Edward to Hertford with a detachment from his own guard, and Princess Mary to Beaulieu. With all the panic and confusion I forgot to mention our New Year's Day presents. I received a minstrel! An Italian quite gifted on the lute. And Edward got yet another jeweled sword and a crossbow. He can barely lift the crossbow. But Father dreams of Edward as a skilled huntsman. Alas, it is not to be. Edward is all brains and very slow with anything in the nature of sporting.

January 18, 1546
Hatfield

We are settled in at Hatfield. One cannot imagine the contortions that we were all put through by Kat checking for poison. This has turned her entire world upside down and inside out. I can tell that dear John Ashley is quite concerned about her. Kat says she shall never eat a Twelfth Night cake again, which is about the stupidest thing I ever heard. How is one to know that a Twelfth Night cake was what caused the Duchess of Lexford's death?

January 19, 1546

I have thought deeply about the Duchess's murder. Robin was whisked away by his father the morning after the Duchess was discovered in the Chapel. So I never got a chance to talk with him about it. But I certainly have my theories of which I write for the first time. I did not even want to write at Greenwich. Who knows what spies might be about? I am more secure here at Hatfield. Rumor says that what ever it was that the Duchess ate or drank was laced with *venin de crapaud*. This is a poison made from the distilled liquids of toads that have been first killed with arsenic. It brings death within hours. I think I do remember the Duchess dancing after the banquet. So she was there for a while. My question is, why did she go to the Chapel? Was it for a meeting with Lord Arran? Mary Ward had seen them embracing in a small chamber off the Chapel that one time. But certainly they would not kiss passionately in a Chapel! This goes beyond being a reformer! And then there is a question of who did it? I, at first, thought the obvious: the Lizard. But is that <u>too</u> obvious?

January 23, 1546

Thank goodness I have my minstrel and William Allen in addition to Master Grindal, or my life would be exceedingly boring with no children here. Kat is still not faring well. So John Ashley, William Allen, and the minstrel Luciano and I play Gleek. But I miss Kat at the card table, she is a shrewd player.

January 26, 1546

A letter from the Queen inquiring about my studies. Do I detect something unsettled in her tone? I think perhaps the poisoning still disturbs us all in a deeper way than we might imagine. I shall be glad when this month is through. I always think that we turn the corner of the season when Candlemas Day comes on February 2.

February 1, 1546

It is one of those teasing winter days that masquerades as spring. The sun comes out full bright. The clouds scuttle off, leaving a glorious blue bowl. But of course there is mud everywhere. However, John Ashley just came and bid me to dress for hawking. He brought his hawks with him. What a treat! Master Grindal releases me from Cicero! But here is the joke. One of John Ashley's hawks is named Cicero.

Later

There is nothing as exhilarating as seeing a superb, long-winged hawk carve great arcs in a flawless sky. The bird seems to draw your spirit with him. I told John that we should have brought Kat out. It would do her so much better than that tincture of poppy she is always dabbing on her tongue when she becomes agitated. He agrees.

February 10, 1546

I received this day a letter from Prince Edward. He, too, laments his lack of the company of other children.

February 14, 1545

What a lovely surprise on this grayest of Valentine's Days. A messenger arrived late this afternoon with a pouch. And in the pouch was a Valentine for me from Robin! He, too, hates the fact that all of us children are apart. I think of us all so distant and lonely in our separate Palaces. It is as if we are far flung stars in the darkness of the night sky, when together we form such a lovely constellation. I look out the window tonight and see my old friend Orion rising now in the heavens.

February 18, 1546

I still think often of the poisoning of the Duchess of Lexford. I think it is a mystery that shall never be solved. This thought, however, just came to me. The Duchess of Lexford was closely related to the Seymours, and remember, dear diary, how I said that the Seymours were the Lizard's chief rivals. Robin said we must watch out and be protective of the Seymours. But nobody thought of watching out for the Duchess of Lexford. Is it possible that because Lord Arran was attracted to the Duchess that Princess Mary and the Lizard thought he might not marry Mary? And therefore if they poisoned the Duchess, she would not be in the way of Mary's marriage plans? Yes, I am beginning to see a picture here. I do think it was the Lizard who committed murder. I still, however, do not believe he tried to poison me. This was just hysterics on Kat's part. Kat, by the way, seems better these last few days.

March 4, 1546

Sun shines today. We go hawking. And Kat comes with us. I make ready to go now. Must wear my high, oiled-skin boots, as the world is thick with mud.

Later

I am breathless, joyous. We were out on a high sere meadow with the hawks when suddenly in the distance we saw a speck on the horizon. As the speck grew closer we realized there were in fact two specks — two men riding hard and yelling and whooping. As they drew nearer, I heard John Ashley say, "Why, it's Sir Ronald and . . ." Robin! Of course, for Sir Ronald is Robin's father's chief secretary and boon companion as well, and often accompanies Robin. I squealed with delight. But to tell the truth, I would never have recognized Robin. He is at least a half foot taller. And he begins to grow a beard! He leaped from his pony and lifted me high off the ground yelling "Elizabeth! Elizabeth!" Underneath the stubble of a beard he was the same old Robin — still a boy. I think Robin shall be a boy forever, even when he grows gray and old and bent. Oh, I am so happy. I think now things begin to change for the better. The year turns as we approach the longer days. The sun grows stronger. Kat grows stronger, Robin taller, and my heart lightens.

March 12, 1546

We hawk. We hunt. We ride ponies. We do some lessons. These are glorious days. Even when it rains, I care not. Not when Robin is here. It is absolutely impossible for me to ever feel lonely when I am in Robin's presence. He is a true friend, next to whom all others pale by comparison. I am never invisible when I am in the company of Robin.

March 15, 1546

The servitors got out the archery frames today, and Robin and I practiced. Each day is so filled now I am too busy to write.

March 19, 1546

A spot of Cicero. A lot of archery. I am getting better with the crossbow.

March 21, 1546

Master Grindal called me in and spoke to me severely about neglecting my studies. He does not want to send a poor report to the Queen. I am mortified. I have been such a fool since Robin has arrived. I know it. Master Grindal said, "Others, Elizabeth, may squander their minds, but yours is too fine to abuse through neglect." I vow to try harder. When Lady Jane Grey and Prince Edward are here I work harder for they are so diligent. I not only want to keep up with them but surpass them.

March 22, 1546

The other day Robin and I spoke for the first time of the poisoning of the Duchess of Lexford. He agrees with me about the Lizard. He said he has heard his father grumbling privately about the Lizard, too. We must watch him when we go to Windsor for Easter.

March 27, 1546

Robin is quite irritated with me. He says I have done nothing but study, which is the truth for the last two weeks. But I must explain, I do so not only for myself but also for the Queen who supports and encourages me so. Robin said something that rather unnerved me. He said the Queen should mind less her own studies. As the words slipped out of Robin's mouth, he turned an icy gray as if he had misspoken. I wanted to ask what he meant, but I did not press him. I think delay and not acting impulsively is often the best strategy. But I shall find out. I like it not when others criticize Catherine Parr.

April 5, 1546
Windsor Castle

The day after Palm Sunday. Robin and I have both noted that a definite coolness has sprung up between Princess Mary and the Lizard.

April 8, 1546

Today was, of course, Maundy Thursday, and this year Father must wash fifty-four pairs of feet. He is fatter than ever. I was shocked not only by his bulk, but what little hair he has left has not a tinge of red in it anymore. It is completely white. And this year I notice something different. My father looks each beggar in the eye steadily, as if he is seeing a reflection of himself. Perhaps he does, but I notice that a soft, misty look stirs in his eye by the time he has reached the thirteenth beggar, and by the end, tears streak down his cheek. It is both water and tears that wash these beggars' feet.

April 15, 1546

We linger here at Windsor. I was hoping that perhaps we might go once more to Woodstock. We had such a fine time there last autumn with Father and the Queen, but I notice a new formality between them. It worries me. I remember that in the letter I received from Queen Catherine, I had detected something unsettling in her tone. I attributed it to the poisoning of the Duchess then.

But that is not it. Oh, I do fear for Catherine. Queens have not fared well in my father's court.

April 20, 1546

I suppose that worry about the Queen has made me somewhat distracted and subdued. I had not realized it until Robin finally spoke to me. His eyes nearly brimming with tears. "You never speak to me or play with me, Elizabeth, and it is not your studies. What is it?" I suddenly remember what he had said about the Queen: that she should mind less her studies. I had decided not to ask him then, but I knew now was the moment. Robin would do anything for me. So I asked. A shadow crossed his eyes. I reached for his hand. "Dear friend, what is it about the Queen? We have always been honest with each other. You are my dearest friend, perhaps my only true friend."

"Elizabeth, it is said that the King is attracted to another." Something went cold inside me. It felt as if a stone sat in my chest.

"Who?"

"Catherine Brandon, the widow of Charles Brandon."

"I see." I spoke barely conscious of the words. I was

thinking yes, she was young and pretty. She had borne Brandon two sons. No Queen had ever borne my father sons that had lived more than a few days, except for Edward's mother, and she had died twelve days later. It all made sense now. Would he divorce the Queen? We stood in the room where I took my lessons and suddenly it began to spin. When I opened my eyes again, I was on the rushes of the floor. Robin knelt white-faced and trembling next to me. "You fainted!"

"I am fine. I am fine!" I felt as if I were shouting. "Say nothing to anyone about this. About my fainting. About the Queen. Do get me some water. Or better still some ale. I shall be fine." Luckily we were alone. Robin came back within the space of a very few minutes. He handed me the flagon of ale. I took a sip. It was bitter. But it cleared my head and settled my stomach. I turned and looked at Robin fiercely. "The Lizard is behind all of this. Mark my words. But he shall not have his way. There shall not be another Queen that dies in the Court of Henry VIII. I vow this, Robin. I shall save the Queen."

"_We_ shall save the Queen, My Lady."

"You are with me in this, Robin?"

"I am. I shall swear a blood oath."

He took out his knife and right there nicked his thumb. I held out mine and he nicked mine. Then just before we pressed our thumbs together, I said, "This is not like getting married, Robin. You know how I feel about that."

"Yes, Elizabeth." He nodded solemnly. "We are our own Round Table here. We are both knights!"

"Yes!" I replied. And at that moment I was filled with an unspeakable whirl of emotions: fierce pride, utter joy, fear, sadness, a strange kind of longing and yes, a deep anger. I must discipline them all to serve Catherine Parr, my most illustrious and virtuous Queen. My teacher, my mother.

April 25, 1546
Hampton Court

Robin and I keep a vigilant eye out for anything that might signal an ill wind for the Queen. Unfortunately there are many ill winds, and the stench rises already at Hampton Court and not only from the rushes. There is talk every day of heresy, of reformers who do not like that the Church of England still has such rituals from Rome. "Too Popish," they cry, even though Father is the head of the church now and not the Pope. The punishment for heretics is to be burned alive. Kat would have a fit if she knew that I am now speaking once more with Mary Ward, but she is worth her weight in gold with the eyes of a hawk, the hearing of a deer, the nose of a ferret and the stealth of a mouse. She slips invisibly through the corridors and in and out of chambers and apartments. She tells us now that the Lizard has begun a very quiet interrogation of suspected heretics within the Court. They begin with the lower members — minstrels, horse grooms. But today they even took Jane the Bald off to interrogate. In other words, they draw the circle tighter and tighter until they can slip the noose around the Queen's neck.

April 28, 1546

Nearly May Day and I do not even care. Today I heard that a poet and a minstrel were taken to the Tower of London last night by the Lord Chancellor and a detail of his own guardsmen. The men were put on the rack and the Lord Chancellor himself, with his aide Richard Rich, turned the screws to stretch the men until they confessed their heresy, their belief in church other than that which my father heads.

May 3, 1546

May Day has come and gone. I pretended I was sick, for I had no stomach for Maying. They say the Lizard has begun to approach some of the Ladies-in-Waiting, the ones who attend the Queen's reading and study circle. The Queen herself looks pale and frightened. She never seeks me out to ask me about my studies. Speaking of which, I am worried sick about Master Grindal.

May 5, 1546

I have come to a decision about Master Grindal. He must leave the Court for his own safety. I realize now that he is a heretic by the definition of the horrible people like the Lizard and his camp. I shall tell him this tonight. I shall tell him that he must plead family illness. His mother is sick. That is what he must tell them.

May 6, 1546

Master Grindal's mother is already dead, and he has no father and his other relatives live too far away. I tell him he must think of something. How can a man who is so smart be so unimaginative? If nothing else, he must get sick himself. Start limping, I tell him. I shall bash him in the knee if I have to.

May 12, 1546

Oh, I am so happy. Master Grindal really is sick. He looks positively ghastly. He returns to Cambridge immediately. I think he should be safe there.

May 16, 1546

The Queen is red-eyed, as if she has been crying. She excused herself early from a banquet and did not go hunting today. I have never known her to miss a hunt.

May 17, 1546

For the first time in two years, I heard the terrible shrieking of Catherine Howard in the Long Gallery last night. When I rose this morning, I knew at first glance that others had heard it, too. She is back! And with good reason.

Later

Robin came to me this morning. He heard it, too. "Should we do it?" he asked. I looked at him and sighed. "Robin, we cannot play ninepins anymore." "Why not?" he asks. I take him by the sleeve and pull him toward the mirror. "See, Robin," I say, looking at our images. He is six feet tall and I am more than five feet tall now. He has a pale beard and I have this winter begun my monthly courses. "We are no longer children. We cannot play games to quiet her spirit. She would not recognize us anymore."

May 19, 1546

This is the tenth anniversary of the death of my mother. Had she lived, I wonder what she would think of me? I went to the Chapel to pray for her. That is easy — to pray for the dead. What is hard is to pray for the living. To pray for Queen Catherine.

May 24, 1546

We have heard more grievous news today. Anne Askew, who has many connections here in Court, especially with the Seymours and with the Queen's Ladies-in-Waiting, was arrested this very morning and taken to the Tower. She is known for her strong Protestant views. The Lizard ordered her arrest. It is said that the Lizard himself will cross-examine her. Poor woman!

May 25, 1546

There are no ordinary times. It is as if we go through the motions of living. Now that Master Grindal has gone, I impose a course of study for myself and try to follow it, but my mind wanders. I play with Edward and the monkeys. But I move through the day as if in a dream. I feel indeed like one of the mechanical creatures that Ponsby builds for the mummeries; that somewhere hidden levers and cranks are turned to give me a pretense of life and motion. I have not seen the Queen in days. It is said that they interrogate Anne Askew in the Tower for information concerning the Ladies-in-Waiting that can give them leads ultimately to the Queen herself.

May 30, 1546

Whitsunday. We celebrate today the descent of the Holy Spirit on the Apostles. There is no Holy Spirit in this land. I have just heard that they put Anne Askew on the rack and that the Lord Chancellor himself turns the screws as he did for the poet and the minstrel taken last month. They draw the noose tighter. Soon I am sure it will encircle Catherine's neck.

June 4, 1546

We move to Whitehall Palace tomorrow. I try to study Cicero. I wonder how my dear Master Grindal is doing. I told him not to write. Anything he says might be held against him. I, perhaps, am writing my own death warrant, for if this diary is discovered I shall be finished.

June 6, 1546
Whitehall Palace

I hear my father does not fare well. His legs are festering and twice within one week had to be cauterized. He growls at everyone. And now it is said that he growls loudest at Queen Catherine, for she dared to "lecture" him on some point. This was most reckless of her indeed. I can only think that she did this because she is so distracted and filled with anxiety. I know not on what point it was she lectured him. I would guess it was something to do with her religious beliefs, which tend to be somewhat Protestant. She likes not many of the more elaborate parts of the mass that my father has kept in his church. This word came to me by way of Mary Ward. I think Kat knows that Mary and I now speak, but she does nothing about it. She, too, senses perhaps that we must all be alert to the danger that lurks within Court.

June 11, 1546

I was called to the royal apartments today. So was Edward. This is the first time we have seen our father or the Queen in weeks. They were sitting in the garden. My father reading something. He barely raised his head to acknowledge our presence. His new doctor, Thomas Wendy, was there, and both Dr. Wendy and the Queen made a great show of greeting us. Then we sat in the most uncomfortable silence. It seemed as though my father's raspy wheeze drowned out even the bird chatter. There was some talk, and then my father said in a low voice. "You lecture me, Kate!" A chill went through me. The Queen got up and came over. "No, no, Your Majesty, I only spoke of the roses, that is all." To tell the truth I do not know of what they were speaking. I was so relieved when we were finally dismissed.

June 25, 1546

I move through my life like a ghost — a ghost haunting herself perhaps or one looking for another body to live within. Robin tells me to be hopeful. He reminds me of our blood oath. But things seem to move in this inexorable, predestined path. What can I do — I, the invisible Princess, daughter of a witch?

July 4, 1546

Very bad news. John Ashley who keeps some of the books for the households and the Queen's estates has been ordered by the Privy Council to deliver them. All the auditors of the Queen's estates have been told to do likewise. This means, says John, that charges of heresy are to be brought against her. This could be the first step toward her arrest.

July 10, 1546

Robin and I were in the rose garden this afternoon when suddenly we heard a hiss from behind the hedge. It was Thomas Wendy the doctor signaling us. He has just visited Father to change the bandages on his legs. Father told Wendy that the Queen is to be arrested tomorrow!

Robin immediately spoke. "We must warn the Queen. Do the Councillors have copies of the charges?" he asked.

"They must," Wendy replied.

"We can try to get them and give them to the Queen," Robin said.

"It is too risky," I replied. Suddenly I felt a searing stab of pain in my stomach. I bent over and held myself. The stabs of pain were real enough, but I knew that like Master Grindal I had made myself sick with fear, and now I should take advantage of it. Both the doctor and Robin caught me as I began to crumble slowly to the ground. "Call the Queen to my apartment. Tell her I am ill. They will not refuse you, Doctor Wendy."

Later

The Queen has been warned! She came almost immediately to my apartments. Robin was still there. We told her what we had heard. I had fully expected her to faint, but she did not. She pulled herself up to her full height and set her jaw. She looked fierce.

July 11, 1546

The Queen has triumphed! Oh, how I wish I had been there. But I was sick, if you recall. Remember, dear diary, how in my last entry I said how fierce the Queen looked. Well, that is not how she went to the King. He was in the walled garden, and Robin had climbed a tree along the wall outside. Perfectly hidden by foliage, he could see all and hear all. This is what he reported: The Queen rushed to the King's side and fell to her knees. She then began to quote the Letters of Saint Paul about how women must learn to be obedient to their husbands and that women, furthermore, since first creation were made subject to men. But the following were the words that saved her most: "Men being made after the image of God ought to instruct their wives, who would do all their learning from them." And she went on that she of all people wished "to be taught by His Majesty, who was a Prince of such excellent learning and wisdom."

The King, said Robin, then looked her in the face and said quite simply: "Then, Kate, we are friends again." And he embraced her.

Then just as Robin was about to climb down from the tree, he heard the sound of many feet approaching. It was the Lizard with forty guards to arrest the Queen. They burst into the garden and found Father and the Queen embracing. Father then looked up and roared like a bear being baited. "Knave! Fool! Beast! Out of my garden!"

I am so thankful. For the first time in weeks I shall rest and sleep the night through. My Queen is saved. I must now write Master Grindal and ask that he return. We children are all to go to Ashridge for the rest of the summer.

July 20, 1546
Ashridge

One sunny day succeeds the next. We hunt. We hawk. We go boating and fishing. Barnaby Fitzpatrick has come. But I do study very hard. Master Grindal is amazed. I do this not just for myself but as a tribute to Queen Catherine. When she was saved, I vowed I would honor her life with the application of my intellect and a renewed zeal in my studies. Even Robin does not criticize me. He seems to understand.

July 25, 1546

Summer is a quiet time. When the leaves begin to turn, in another month or so, that is when the pace quickens. Father and the Queen go to their hunting lodges. I hope again for a visit with them at Woodstock. If I do not write often now, know that it is because everything in my life is placid yet not boring. I am satisfied and do not need to confide so desperately now as I once did. There are so few pages left in this diary. I must ask Kat for a new one, soon. I shall use the remaining pages sparingly.

December 23, 1546
Enfield

Dear diary, I have done once more what I vowed never to do. Lied to you. I think it is a lie, although some might say that it is a silent lie rather than a written or spoken one. That is why I have written so little until now. A lie nonetheless. It was true as I last wrote that one sunny day succeeded the next. Perhaps the good weather made it all the crueler, but we began to receive reports of my father's failing health. I chose not to write about this. Along with the reports was all the accompanying gossip regarding succession. There were rumors that Mary would be chosen over Edward. For in recent months Father had begun to shower her with jewels. It seemed as if every week throughout the summer I would hear of a new gift being bestowed on Mary. A dread began to build within me. I was in some ways nearly paralyzed with fear. So I chose not to think about it. That is why I have not written.

In early September, we were all most happy when we heard that Father was better and planned his fall hunting trip. We were to join him at the end of it at Woodstock in time for Michaelmas, but then came the news. He was ill again.

Our Michaelmas visit was canceled. Like leaves from a tree, the holidays began to drop away uncelebrated. Michaelmas came and went, Edward's birthday, All Hallows' Eve, and All Souls' Day. Edward, Mary, and I were left to languish in our separate country estates. Again I felt myself becoming the forgotten, invisible Princess. Then more rumors about Mary succeeding the King.

Now it is Christmas. What a strange Christmas it is. There is no Lord of Misrule appointed. I am still here at Enfield without Robin or Barnaby or even Lady Jane. Edward is at Ashridge and Mary at Beaulieu. But most alarming of all even the Queen has been sent away to Greenwich for the Twelve Days of Christmas. My father has never been separated from his wife, any wife, on Christmas. They say he is gravely ill and is kept in utter seclusion in Whitehall Palace in London. They say that he cannot and has not signed his own name for months and that his Privy Councillors use the dry stamp to imprint his signature.

We wait here now. It is a cheerless Christmas. We wait for the death of a King, and I wait for the rest of my life and wonder what will happen. For my life will change, and could change in most unfortunate, nay truly horrid ways.

December 24, 1546

We go to midnight mass for Christmas eve. I pray for my father. And yes, I pray for myself.

December 25, 1546

What a dreary Christmas day, made drearier by Kat and John Ashley's immense efforts to be jolly. I had a horrible dream last night. I dreamed of my father. He appeared grotesquely fat and he had a baffled look in his eyes. He was absently handing jewel after jewel over to Princess Mary, then he looked up at me. His eyes cleared and in this high, yet snarling little voice he began to sing:

> *Robin clad in green did come to see the Queen.*
> *And sitting by the throne*
> *Two Princesses were shone.*
> *Hey, nonny nonny. Hey, nonny nonny.*
> *One in shadows glowed despite her lack of gems.*
> *The other in the sun looked verily so glum . . .*

It was the ditty for which I was banished from court nearly three summers ago at Greenwich. I fear this dream is an omen.

January 18, 1547

The year turned. We hear no new news of Father. No letters from the Queen nor from Edward. I would not expect any from Robin as he never writes. Perhaps from Lady Jane, but now I have reasoned that she is scared to write me. That she knows something about the succession that I do not. She knows Princess Mary for her true self and rumors of Mary's succession would be enough to frighten Jane into silence. It could even be dangerous for her to write. I am no fool. We must all look after ourselves at certain times.

January 19, 1546

I must stop wallowing in fear and self-pity. I have decided to train my mind on other things, for even my studies do not distract me from my worries. Here is what I have made myself focus on. A barn swallow. Or at least that is what John Ashley says the little drab-colored bird that begins to make a nest outside my window is. I say, why is it called a barn swallow if it nests here on my window ledge? He says it must be drawn to something at this window, this corner of Enfield. "Maybe to you, Princess." Today in the course of the morning she has a nest half-built.

January 21, 1547

The barn swallow's nest is all built. I watched yesterday as she dug her tiny beak into the downy fluff under her outer feathers and plucked some to tuck into her nest. Imagine such poverty that one must pluck from one's own body to build one's home and shelter. I look around my own apartments, at the tapestries woven with tales from Greek mythology, the inlaid ivory desk, and the tasseled embroidery table covers.

January 28, 1547

Joy! Three speckled eggs lay so cozily in the swallow's nest! To me they seem to sparkle as splendidly as gems on this dull January day.

January 29, 1547

I hear wonderful news today. Edward is to arrive tomorrow from Ashridge. I am so excited.

January 31, 1547

Dear diary, I can hardly believe these words that I am about to inscribe. My father, King Henry VIII, is dead. He died in the small hours of the morning of January 28, the very same morning when I discovered the swallow's eggs. They kept his death a secret from the whole world for three days. I know not why. Edward Seymour, who had brought Edward here, told us this morning. He came to my apartments and asked that Edward be brought and that John and Kat Ashley be there. Edward and I both burst into tears as he told us. I pressed my hands to my eyes for I do not know how long, perhaps many seconds, or two or three minutes. I could hear Edward sniffling and gulping and then there seemed to be silence. Next I heard a voice say, "Long live the King," and when I took my hands down from my face, I noticed that Edward Seymour and Kat and John Ashley were all kneeling in front of Edward. My brother is King! My brother and not Princess Mary. I sank to my knees as much in relief as homage.

February 1, 1547

I am still in a state of disbelief. Father is dead and my nine-year-old brother is King. Today Edward was taken to London, where his uncle Edward Seymour is to be recognized officially as my brother's protector.

P.S. I guess now Barnaby Fitzpatrick's wish will come true. He shall be the whipping boy!

February 5, 1547

I am often the last to hear what is to happen. I now am told to make ready to be conveyed to London immediately. My father's body lies in state in Whitehall. We children shall go there to mourn him. It remains to be seen if Princess Mary and I shall attend the funeral. It is the custom that the new King never attend the funeral of the old one. The funeral is to be at Windsor. Father is to be buried in a magnificent tomb next to Jane Seymour in Saint George's Chapel. I wonder how Queen Catherine feels about this.

February 10, 1547
Whitehall Palace

Tonight Princess Mary, Edward, and I go to the Chapel Royal, which will be cleared of mourners so we may pay our last love and honor to our father. I am afraid.

Later

A thousand or more tapers burned. Will Somers came with us. For this I am most glad. I like Will because he answers all of our questions so straightforwardly, unlike many adults. When Edward said, "The coffin is so large even for one my father's size," Will explained that Father rested in a smaller coffin that was contained within this larger one. This outer coffin was draped in black and had precious stones set in its top. There were many banners as well that draped it. The coffin rested beneath a canopy of sheer gold fabric through which the light of the tapers was filtered, like the light of many very distant suns. On an empty coffin next to my father's they have made a wax replica of him gowned in velvet robes just like the ones he wore, and covered with jewels. I said the prayers for the dead but I barely felt the words on my lips. All I could think about was Father's body in the huge box. I could not concentrate on my prayers at all.

February 13, 1547

Today they remove the coffin to convey it to Windsor. It shall take at least two days. The coffin itself reaches nine stories high when put on the hearse and weighs more than a ton. The road is icy and rutted. I am not to attend the funeral. Nor is Mary.

February 16, 1547

The funeral is today. We children remain here at Whitehall. Edward, of course, is busy as he shall be crowned in exactly four days. Westminster Abbey is made ready. Robes are being made. Edward is given lessons on how to walk, how to hold the scepter, how to hold his head so it will not tire from the weight of the·crown. Princess Mary plays cards ceaselessly. I wonder about my little swallow back at Enfield.

February 28, 1547

I have returned to Enfield. Edward is now crowned King, sovereign of the realm. He performed magnificently throughout the whole long ceremony. Everyone commented on his great dignity. His head never wobbled as the Archbishop set on the crown. Edward looked like an angel dressed in cloth of silver with diamonds and rubies. But an angel, I noticed, with a slightly drippy nose. Edward always seems to have a little sniffle, and it is very hard to fetch one's handkerchief and wipe one's nose when holding swords, scepters, and maces and bearing a crown. I pray now every evening and morning for my brother's health. May his nose stop running. May he grow lean and strong. For verily my life depends on it.

March 3, 1547

The eggs have begun to hatch. I have watched all morning. Suddenly within the last few minutes, I spy a naked pink little thing. Its beak poking up. In a few minutes it is hatched. The baby bird looks no bigger than a fat worm. I feel such joy swell within me as I witness this. I remember when I first discovered the swallow and marveled at a creature of such poverty that it needed to pluck from its own body to make its shelter. And yet now I look at this mother swallow and her baby no bigger than a fat worm, and I think, I am a Princess, often a forgotten one, yet there but for the grace of God go I. In other words why was I born a Princess and not a bird? And for one sliver of a second I think perhaps I would trade places with this creature and then be free to wheel through the skies and be forever rich in ways I cannot imagine. I shall not lie, dear diary, never again. It is more than a sliver of a thought. And I know I shall return to it again and again and again. Would I trade my title for a bird's life, a palace for a nest, a realm for the sky?

Epilogue

Elizabeth's belief in her destiny to become queen was to be fulfilled, but not for another eleven years after the death of her father. However, at no time in her life were her courage and wits put to a more severe test than in those next eleven years.

Shortly after King Henry VIII's death, Catherine Parr married Thomas Seymour, whose brother, Edward Seymour, was the regent for Edward, who was now the king of England. Catherine Parr died in 1548 and Thomas Seymour was arrested almost immediately for treason and for plotting to marry Elizabeth. Elizabeth was questioned harshly by members of the Privy Council, as were her servants. Kat Ashley was even imprisoned in the Tower for a short time. When Elizabeth was informed of the beheading of Thomas Seymour, she betrayed no emotion whatsoever, if indeed she had ever been in love with him. However, this ordeal was nothing in comparison to what would follow.

In 1553, Edward the VI, always a frail and sickly boy, died. Now Princess Mary became queen, and never was Elizabeth's life in more danger than during Mary's reign. Within a short time after being crowned queen, Mary became known as Bloody Mary, for she was bent on making England Catholic and burned many at the stake who were not. Elizabeth pretended to be a Catholic in order to save her own life. But at this time, there were many Protestants plotting against the Catholic queen. Mary, fearing that Princess Elizabeth would become the focus of an attempt to remove her from her throne, had Elizabeth arrested and sent to the Tower. Elizabeth was only in the Tower for a short time. Soon after, she was put under house arrest at her father's old hunting lodge, Woodstock. Mary died childless five years later. So in 1558, at the age of twenty-five, Elizabeth became queen.

England was jubilant about their pretty and lively new queen. She was both majestic and modest. She assured the people that under her rule there would be no more burnings because of religious beliefs. Still, people wanted

Protestantism to be officially restored. In 1559 the Act of Supremacy passed by Parliament declared the queen the supreme governor of the Church of England, while the Act of Uniformity established a version of an older prayer book as the one to be used in church services. Even after the passage of these acts, Elizabeth stated clearly that she would not "open windows in men's souls," meaning that she did not care to peer into the private beliefs that individual people might have about God.

Elizabeth remained good friends with Robin Dudley. Her councillors were constantly trying to get her to marry. King Philip II of Spain, Queen Mary's widower husband, proposed, as did the son of the French king, but Elizabeth would have none of them. She finally said to one of her councillors, who was insisting on her marrying, "I will have here but one mistress and no master." She indeed became known as the Virgin Queen, who was wedded only to her kingdom, England.

Elizabeth was a very good politician. She was not only able to deal with rival factions within her own country but for years played a delicate game of balancing England's interests against those of France and Spain. Perhaps the greatest moment in her long reign was England's defeat of the supposedly invincible Spanish Armada in 1588.

At the time that Elizabeth lived and was Queen, women were expected to marry. They were not permitted to speak out on issues in public, nor were they educated. Elizabeth was a woman who as queen lived in defiance of what the world expected or considered to be proper for a woman. She never married, she spoke out and made policy, she wrote and translated poetry, and she published those writings.

Her reign of nearly forty-five years was a glorious one in which she continued to play politics, make brilliant speeches, flirt with her admirers, and parry with her councillors. She encouraged the arts, and within her court, a playwright named William Shakespeare presented some of his first plays. Elizabeth I ruled with a blend of craft, grace, shrewdness, and majesty. She became the glittering emblem of an age that was stamped so indelibly by her personality that it became known as the Elizabethan Age. Good Queen Bess became the ultimate image of majestic and powerful female authority. She died in her seventieth year on March 24, 1603.

Life in the Tudor Court

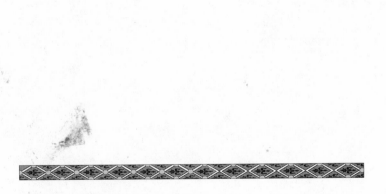

Historical Note

Princess Elizabeth's grandfather — Henry VII, who founded the House of Tudor — reigned during a time of amazing changes in Europe, 1509–1547. In 1492, Christopher Columbus discovered a new world — America. Soon European ships, with Spain and Portugal in the lead, were sailing regularly around the globe. They brought back wondrous goods: silk, cotton, porcelain, rugs, gold, silver, sugar, and spices. Meanwhile the widespread production of muskets and cannons transformed warfare. Armored knights on horseback had no defense against gunpowder. They became relics of the past who appeared in stories and games. Printing presses with movable type made books widely available. Until then, only the clergy and the wealthy knew how to read or could afford to buy a single book. By 1530, about sixty percent of all English people could read.

Henry VII died in 1509. Some historians say he had an unpleasant personality and a miserly character, but he gave England a precious gift: a more stable future. He left the royal treasury full of money, and he provided the House of Tudor with a male heir — his son Henry.

Henry VIII ascended the throne when he was just eighteen years old. He was handsome — tall with red hair and a red beard. Henry not only supported the work of artists, he wrote poetry and music himself. He set up a brilliant and luxurious court where he entertained and governed. He had inherited sixteen palaces in and around London. He bought and built others.

Unlike his father, Henry VIII spent money easily, too easily. His high living and ill-fated wars with France drained the royal treasury. He had to devalue the coinage twice. This meant he created more coins by adding copper to the available silver. Each new coin had less real value than an old one. An image of the king's face was stamped on the coins. When the reddish copper showed through the silver, the people called Henry "old copper nose" and said he was blushing for shame.

During Henry's reign, a religious upheaval called the Reformation spread across Europe. Until then, the overwhelming majority of Europeans belonged to the Catholic Church. Its supreme authority was the Pope in Rome. The Catholic Church had great power and wealth. It owned vast lands and thousands of magnificent buildings — palaces as well as churches — filled with art treasures. Many high church officials lived in luxury like kings. Many were corrupt.

In order to create a pure church, various reform movements sprang up. Each group had its own philosophy. Each believed it had the one and only religious truth. Yet they all considered themselves "Protestants"— they *protested* the moral decline of the Catholic Church. These Protestants rejected the authority of the Pope. They believed in a direct relationship between Christians and their god. They rejected Latin, the language of the Catholic mass. Instead, they wanted worshipers to pray in whatever language they normally spoke.

Such reforms did not come about peacefully. The Catholic Church condemned Protestants as heretics and was willing to burn them at the stake. Fighting, even civil wars, broke out.

In England, the conflict between Catholics and Protestants had a unique twist: Henry VIII severed all ties to the Pope and the Catholic Church because he wanted to divorce his wife, Catherine of Aragon, who had not given him a male heir. Catholics were not allowed to divorce, so Henry asked the Pope for special permission. When the Pope refused, Henry declared himself the supreme head of an independent national church of England. In 1534, the English Parliament confirmed Henry's declaration.

Free to divorce and remarry, Henry had a total of six wives who produced a total of three children: Mary, the daughter of Catherine of Aragon, Elizabeth, the daughter of Anne Boleyn, and Edward, the son of Jane Seymour. The break with the Pope also gave Henry the opportunity to seize the immense property of the Catholic Church. He gave parcels of land to noble followers in order to create a landed aristocracy loyal to the House of Tudor. He put the rest of the wealth into the royal treasury and spent it.

The creation of a national church did not prevent religious conflict in England. On the contrary, it launched a period of confusion and bloodshed. When Henry died in 1547, nine-year-old Edward VI took the throne. Edward and the men who helped him rule pushed England toward a more radical Protestantism. When Edward died just six years later, Mary Tudor, a devout Catholic, became queen.

Mary's reign lasted only five years. When she died in 1558, twenty-five-year-old Elizabeth took the throne. She faced great dangers. England was almost bankrupt. Rising prices made life miserable for the poor. One great enemy, Spain, controlled the Netherlands just across the English Channel. Another great enemy, France, controlled Scotland, just north of England. Spain, France, and the English Catholics plotted constantly to get rid of Elizabeth. They wanted to put the young Catholic Mary Stuart, Queen of Scots, on the English throne. Few people expected Elizabeth to survive this situation.

Elizabeth did survive. She proved herself intelligent and skillful in the art of politics. She was the leader of the Church of England, but she made church teachings loose enough so that most of the population felt comfortable. Elizabeth chose talented advisers who served her well for decades. She put finances on a more solid basis.

In foreign policy, Elizabeth dealt with the French menace early on. In 1559, she sent her army and fleet to help the Protestants in Scotland drive out the French for good.

Spain continued to threaten England until the great Spanish Armada, a fleet of 130 ships carrying 30,000 men and 2,400 guns, sailed into the English Channel in 1588. The Spanish planned to invade England, get rid of Elizabeth, and reestablish the Catholic Church. Instead, 200 smaller but faster English ships battered the Spanish until a huge storm blew the Armada north and around Scotland where more than half the ships sank.

Although the war with Spain dragged on, England no longer felt threatened. Confidence and national pride soared. The population adored Queen Elizabeth, who had successfully steered England past one difficulty after another. For her subjects, Elizabeth symbolized England. She embodied the best of their beloved island nation.

After defeating the Armada, England was freer to explore the seas, regulate trade with distant lands, and even begin planning a first colony in America. This time of exuberant national spirit coincided with an upsurge in artistic creativity. Great writers, including William Shakespeare, Edmund Spenser, Christopher Marlowe, Francis Bacon, Ben Jonson, and John Donne, worked during the later years of Elizabeth's reign. Musicians gave England her greatest prominence ever in this field. Elizabeth spent little money on palaces, but she loved jewelry and clothes. Her interest spurred craftspeople to develop their arts.

Elizabeth never married, but she used the possibility of marriage as a political tool. She would hint at her willingness to marry into a foreign royal family, yet she never followed through on these hints. She believed her independence gave her greater strength and actually allowed her to rule.

Elizabeth reigned for nearly forty-five years. She refused to name an heir to the throne, but when she died in 1603, her advisers managed a peaceful transition. The Protestant son of Mary, Queen of Scots, was crowned King James I of England. He was the first king of a new dynasty — the House of Stuart.

Elizabeth left her successor some serious problems: inadequate tax revenues, no army for national defense, and weak local governments. She also left a legacy of political stability, economic expansion, a successful religious reformation, the elimination of Spain and France as threats to England, and the unification of the English nation. Most people believed that young Princess Elizabeth would never be queen. She proved them wrong and gave her name to a crucial period in English history — the Elizabethan Age.

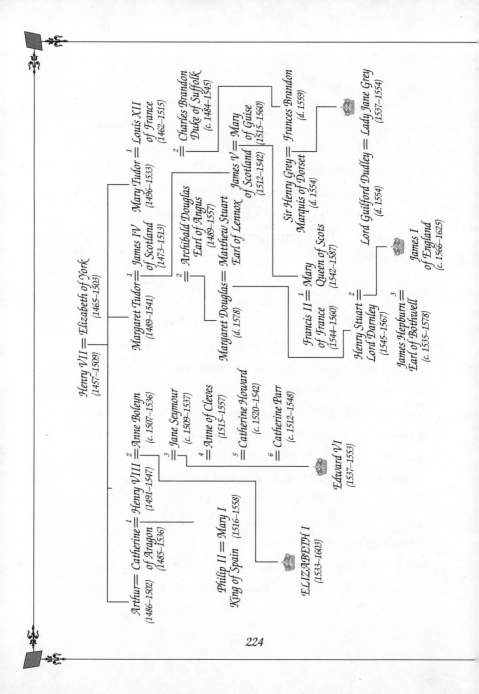

Henry VII = Elizabeth of York
(1457–1509)   (1465–1503)

Arthur = Catherine ¹= Henry VIII ²= Anne Boleyn
(1486–1502) of Aragon (1491–1547) (c. 1507–1536)
(1485–1536)

³= Jane Seymour
(c. 1509–1537)

⁴= Anne of Cleves
(1515–1557)

⁵= Catherine Howard
(c. 1520–1542)

⁶= Catherine Parr
(c. 1512–1548)

Philip II = Mary I (1516–1558)
King of Spain

ELIZABETH I
(1533–1603)

Edward VI
(1537–1553)

Margaret Tudor ¹= James IV   Mary Tudor ¹= Louis XII
(1489–1541)   of Scotland (1496–1533) of France
                (1473–1513)   (1462–1515)

Archibald Douglas
Earl of Angus
(1489–1557)

²=   ²= Charles Brandon
                          Duke of Suffolk
                          (c. 1484–1545)

Matthew Stuart James V = Mary
Earl of Lennox of Scotland of Guise
                (1512–1542) (1515–1560)

Margaret Douglas
(d. 1578)

Sir Henry Grey = Frances Brandon
Marquis of Dorset (d. 1559)
(d. 1554)

Francis II ¹= Mary
of France   Queen of Scots
(1544–1560)   (1542–1587)

Henry Stuart ²=
Lord Darnley
(1545–1567)

James Hepburn ³=
Earl of Bothwell
(c. 1535–1578)

Lord Guilford Dudley = Lady Jane Grey
(d. 1554)   (1537–1554)

James I
of England
(c. 1566–1625)

The Tudor Family Tree

The British Tudor dynasty began with Henry Tudor, crowned Henry VII in 1485. Henry VII married Elizabeth of York, the eldest daughter of Edward IV, in 1486. Their union produced four children who survived childhood: Arthur, Henry VIII, Margaret Tudor, and Mary Tudor. The chart illustrates the growth of the dynasty through 1625. The crown symbol indicates those who reigned over England. Double lines represent marriages; single lines indicate parentage. Dates of births and deaths (where available) are noted.

Henry VIII: Henry became King of England in 1509 at age seventeen. He died in 1547 after a thirty-eight year reign.

Henry VIII's Children

Mary I: The daughter of Henry VIII and Catherine of Aragon, Mary I was Queen of England from 1553 to 1558.

Elizabeth I: The only child of Henry VIII and Anne Boleyn, Elizabeth I ascended the throne of England in 1558 and ruled until 1603.

Edward VI: The only heir of Henry VIII and Jane Seymour, Edward VI ruled England from 1547 to 1553.

Henry VIII's Wives

1 *Catherine of Aragon:* She was the widow of Henry's older brother, Arthur. Her parents, King Ferdinand and Queen Isabella of Spain, consented to her marrying Henry in 1509. They had one child, Mary Tudor.

2 *Anne Boleyn:* Henry married Anne in 1533, though his marriage to Catherine was not yet annulled. Anne gave birth to their daughter, Elizabeth, on September 7, 1533. Falsely accused of adultery, Anne was beheaded.

3 *Jane Seymour:* She married Henry on May 30, 1536, only eleven days after Anne Boleyn was executed. On October 12, 1537, she gave birth to Henry's only male heir, Edward VI. She died a few days after Edward's birth.

4 *Anne of Cleves:* The daughter of Germany's Duke of Cleves, she married Henry on January 6, 1540. It was a marriage of political convenience for Henry, and the marriage was annulled six months later.

5 *Catherine Howard:* Catherine, Anne Boleyn's first cousin, became Henry's wife in 1540, shortly after the annulment of his previous marriage. Found guilty of adultery, Catherine was imprisoned in the Tower of London and beheaded.

6 *Catherine Parr:* She was a widow of four months when Henry became her third husband on July 12, 1543. They remained wed until Henry's death on January 28, 1547.

King Henry VIII's power and majesty is conveyed in this engraving of a portrait painted in 1540 by Hans Holbein the Younger. Holbein painted the monarch in a manner so lifelike, the King's eyes and limbs actually seemed to move.

Assisted by advisers, Edward ruled England from the age of nine until his death from tuberculosis in July 1553.

An innocent-looking Mary I, seen here at age twenty-eight. Nine years later, she would be known as Bloody Mary for the violent persecution of Protestants under her rule.

The future Queen of England, Elizabeth I, at about age thirteen.

Elizabeth's coronation portrait. Wearing a jeweled crown and an exquisite robe of cloth-of-gold lined with ermine, she holds the orb and scepter, symbols of her imperial and absolute power.

Once a royal residence and a prison, the Tower of London on the north bank of the Thames River is now a popular tourist attraction. This view of the Tower shows the Traitor's Gate, where many prisoners, including Elizabeth I, entered the fortress.

A photograph of the well-preserved Hatfield House. During her childhood, Elizabeth was often exiled to this palace nestled in the secluded English countryside.

.... cv work cop to have finn plugto by queen elizabeth.

*Though it was not her
favorite pastime,
Elizabeth was skilled
at needlework.
The cover of this book from the
British Museum is credited
as her handiwork.*

31 Et aucunesfois ie propose a mõ pouoir dy resister, mais quant vn peu de tribulacion m aduiet ce m est tresgrand et griesue an goisse et de bien peu de chose sesleue tresgrande tentacion 32 Car quant ie pense estre asseur et fort, et que ainsy quil me sem ble ray laduantage soudaine ment par vn petit tourbillon du vent de tentacion.ie me sens prest de tumber 33 Pourtant o seigneur regarde mon impotence.et considere ma	fragilité laquelle tu congnois le mieulx 34 Ayes mercy de moy.et me delyure de tout peche et iniqui te acellefin que ie ne soye acca blé diceux 35 Il m est souuentesfois fort en nuy. et cela quasi me consond.de ce que ie suis sy instable sy fee ble et fragile pour resister aux motions iniques lesquelles.cõ bien quelles ne me causent de consentir.ce nonobstant me sõt leurs assaulx tresgriefz.

*These pages, dated December 30, 1545, are taken from a book of prayers that
Elizabeth at age twelve translated into Latin, French, and Italian as a New Year's
gift to her father. The prayers were composed by her stepmother Catherine Parr.*

Elizabeth I died in London on March 23, 1603. This magnificent marble effigy in her image rests on top of her tomb at Westminster Abbey.

About the Author

Kathy Lasky says, "I loved writing the diary of Elizabeth. I chose to cover the years when she was just about the age I was when I was learning English history. As always the most fun for me was doing the research. I spend endless hours finding out about how often, or not often enough, they took baths. I loved all those little gross details about wig bug and rats in the palaces. But, of course, I loved the glitter and dazzle. After all the research was done, I would find myself wondering sometimes how confounding it must have been for a young girl, whether she was a princess or not, to sometimes be loved and then sometimes be sent away by one's father. How hard it must have been to know that your mother's head had actually been cut off by command of your father. These were musings that could never be answered directly in history books. So although historians may say that Elizabeth was always strong, or that at worst she might in her old age have suffered 'occasional bouts of melancholia' or depression, they do not know for sure. They never will, and this is why it is so much fun to write a fictional diary for a real princess. I had done my research as thoroughly as any scholar, but because this is fiction I could, based on what I found, try to responsibly imagine the loneliness, the fears, and the joys of a Princess."

Acknowledgments

Cover painting by Tim O'Brien

Page 227: Portrait of Henry VIII and his wives, Corbis-Bettman, New York, New York.

Page 228: King Henry VIII standing, Corbis-Bettman, New York, New York.

Page 229 (top): Edward VI, North Wind Picture Archives, Alfred, Maine.

Page 229 (bottom): Mary I, North Wind Picture Archives, Alfred, Maine.

Page 230: Elizabeth I as young princess, The Granger Collection, New York, New York.

Page 231: Queen Elizabeth I in coronation robes, The Granger Collection, New York, New York.

Page 232 (top): Traitors' Gate, Tower of London, The Bridgeman Art Library, London.

Page 232 (bottom): Hatfield House, The Bridgeman Art Library, London.

Page 233 (top): Needlework book cover, North Wind Picture Archives, Alfred, Maine.

Page 233 (bottom): Translated prayers by Queen Elizabeth I, The Granger Collection, New York, New York.

Page 234: Marble effigy of Queen Elizabeth I, The Granger Collection, New York, New York.

Lasky, Kathryn.
Elizabeth I, red rose of the House of Tudor / by Kathryn Lasky.
cm.—(The royal diaries)
Summary: In a series of diary entries, Princess Elizabeth, the eleven-year-old
daughter of King Henry VIII, celebrates holidays and birthdays, relives her
mother's execution, revels in her studies, and agonizes over her father's health.
ISBN 0-590-68484-1
1. Elizabeth I, Queen of England, 1533–1603—Childhood and youth—
Juvenile fiction.   2. Great Britain—History—Henry VIII, 1509–1547—
Juvenile fiction.   [1. Elizabeth I, Queen of England, 1533–1603—
Childhood and youth—Fiction. 2. Great Britain—History—Henry VIII,
1509–1547—Fiction. 3. Princesses—Fiction. 4. Diaries—Fiction.] I. Title.
II. Series.
PZ7.L3274E1 1999
[Fic]—dc21   99-11178

CIPISBN 0-590-68484-1

12 11 10 9 8 7 6 5 4 3 2 1   9/9 0/0 01 02 03 04

The display type was set in Zapf Chancery.
The text type was set in Augereau.
Book design by Elizabeth B. Parisi
Printed in the U.S.A.   23
First printing, June 1999
♦♦